Crime

is of the

Essence

Crime
is of the
Essence

JOE CSIDA

COACHWHIP PUBLICATIONS
Greenville, Ohio

To the women in my life:
Ma, Monkey, and Skook

Crime is of the Essence, by Joe Csida
© 2021 Coachwhip Publications edition

Cover image: Perfume bottle © ElliVelli; texture © Paul
   Grand and Jill Ferry

First published 1947
Joseph Csida, 1912-1996. Joe Csida was an author, musi-
   cian, personal manager, and editor of *Billboard,* along
   with other pursuits in the recording and entertainment industries.
CoachwhipBooks.com

ISBN 1-61646-507-7
ISBN-13 978-1-61646-507-0

1

What it was I didn't know, but it went ummmuumm, ummmmuummm, like somebody with a strong throat and a good nose endlessly humming a monotonous, two-noted tune. I turned the knob and pushed, but the door, as I had expected, was locked. I knocked. The humming noise died down and he said, "Yes?"

"Please," I said, "stop kibitzing and come on downstairs. "I've got to see you about the show."

"Presently, Shelley. I'm busy at the moment."

The humming sound started again and I turned disgustedly and walked toward the stairs. I wondered about the sound, but only a little. After you've been wondering about something practically every day for six years, you get a little tired of it. I'd been with Mr. Tinney that long, and in the beginning I'd kept after him to tell me what the noise was. He never would.

It always came from behind the locked door of his own room, so, on the few occasions I'd been in there, I'd looked around but I'd never seen anything to account for it.

At the moment I had other things to think about. Wakely was raising hell. On last night's broadcast, Mr. Tinney had become so interested in Case Number X-46315 he'd refused to let the announcer do the closing commercial. On the same show a middle-aged woman with eight children had referred to a certain gentleman disparagingly and by name. The gentleman was threatening to sue Wakely for twenty-five thousand dollars.

Downstairs, in the combination library-office, I plopped into my favorite chair and picked up Millay's *Wine from These Grapes* again, I looked at my watch. Three forty-six. In another fourteen minutes Little Miss Trouble was due.

I resigned myself to the fact that I wasn't going to be able to discuss the program with Mr. Tinney till after she left. I turned the pages of *Wine,* and thought about her. She was Carol Wills and no worse, I suppose, than any one of the hundreds of other people with messed-up lives who came to Mr. Tinney for counsel. I liked her, in fact. It was just that hers was the first problem I'd actually seen Mr. Tinney work on.

Five years earlier, at the age of eighteen, she'd come to New York, fresh from Twin Whip, Idaho (population, 835), looking for a job and romance. She had found both. The job, typist in a wholesale drug supply house; the romance in a ballroom on Broadway between Fifty-third and Fifty-fourth Streets. Here she met Jimmy Knight. Jimmy was young, handsome, and first sax in the ballroom's band. He was also weak-willed and a hophead, although Carol didn't become aware of these last two characteristics until six months after she'd become Mrs. Knight, which was a little less than two months after she met him.

Even after she found out, she stuck with him, partly because she thought she loved him, but more because he needed her. Jimmy started peddling dope. To celebrate their first wedding anniversary he came home with a couple of fellows—detectives from the Narcotics Bureau, one on either side of him. He had hidden in a hat box of Carol's a couple of decks of cocaine, two pint bottles of Cannabis Indica (which, mixed with ordinary tobacco, makes a good reefer) and a couple of boxes of home-made marijuanas.

In trying to beat the rap, the gallant Knight almost had Carol sent to prison. Almost, but not quite. He involved her only enough to cause her to lose her job, while he himself was sentenced to Sing Sing for three to ten years.

In the middle of all this mess Carol heard from a friend who'd heard from a friend about Mr. Tinney, human relations counsellor, and came to him. Maybe it was his maneuverings which kept her from going to jail. I do know that he got her marriage to James Knight annulled.

My thoughts were shattered by a loud banging noise from the kitchen.

"Hey, Mamie," I yelled, "you dropped your watch."

"I'll thank you to mind your own business, Shelley," Mamie yelled back.

I flipped the pages of Millay's book, but couldn't revive my interest in it, so I put it back on the table and thought about Carol again.

After Knight, she was a heartsore little girl for a long, long time. She got another job finally with Siquin, Incorporated, a perfume house, and did well. She worked hard and one of the owners, Randolph Kerwin, made her his personal secretary.

Then, about a year ago, along came love—again! This time she fell for the boss' son. Not her boss', his partner's. A boy called Ben Sikkim. Ben was all right—a clean, earnest, ambitious kid and nuts about Carol. It began to look like maybe she'd hit Cupid's jackpot. And then Ben's old man decided nix.

He was really something, the old man. A Brahman, a high-caste, well-educated Indian from Bombay, with very definite ideas about who was master of the house and what's good and no good for his offspring.

According to Carol, he wasn't going to stop at anything to prevent Ben from marrying her. He'd told her he'd toss Ben out on his ear if he married her. That would have put a real dent in the kid's ambition, which was to be a doctor. He still had two years more to go at college. He was willing to chuck it and get a job and study nights, but Carol couldn't see it. She figured that after a while the pace would get too tough and Ben might have to give up the idea of becoming a doctor, and in later years he might feel it was her fault.

All this had happened quite recently, and Carol, who'd kept up her friendship with us, had come and told Mr. Tinney about it. He was mulling it over and trying to figure out a solution.

I'd mulled it over, too, but why old man Sikkim should have become so dead set against the marriage all of a sudden was way over my head. I'm not especially good at problems, anyway. That's Mr. Tinney's job. I'm still just an "artist's representative," which is fancy for personal manager. I used to handle bands and singers and once even a ventriloquist. I'd given them all up to handle Mr. Tinney.

For one thing, I liked the old egomaniac and honestly felt he was doing an honest-to-goodness human service. For another, I felt he was worth plenty of money as an entertainment attraction and I was the boy to sell him. Which I had, as witness the fifteen-hundred-dollar-a-week *Wakely Soapchips* broadcasts. The trouble was he took plenty of handling.

Mamie walked in from the kitchen then, bearing a tray—the one Mr. Tinney claims he got from a Chinaman during the Boxer Rebellion—with a tea pot, cup and saucer, and a plate of cookies on it. She set it down on the table in front of the fireplace.

"Mamie," I said, "how sweet of you!"

"This isn't for you, Shelley, and you know it. It's for Miss Wills."

Sure I knew it. Carol was one of Mamie's pets and I most definitely was not. Mamie thought I'd "forced" Mr.

Tinney into the unthinkable idea of broadcasting his clients' troubles to millions of morbid morons. She'd always resented me.

She started back to the kitchen.

"Hey, Mamie, when was Carol here last?"

"About a week ago, if it's any of your business."

"Is she still having trouble with Ben's old man?"

She shook her large gray head woefully. "More than ever. Mr. Sikkim must be a fiend. That poor child has seen more grief in her twenty-three years than most people see in a lifetime."

"Maybe she's lucky at cards," I plagued Mamie.

"What have cards to do with it?" She scowled.

"You know, lucky at cards, unlucky at love."

"Shelley, you're a fiend." It was one of her favorite words.

The doorbell chimed and I started to get up, but Mamie hustled her two hundred and sixty pounds through the living room and foyer.

"Hello, darlin'," she said.

"Hello, Mrs. Hannigan."

Voices are funny. Here, Carol Wills was still at the door and all she'd said was hello and I knew she wasn't happy. There was a haunted note in her voice, haunted and weary, like someone who's had nightmares every night for a week.

"Come and sit down, child," Mamie said, leading her to a chair opposite mine in the library-office. "I've just brewed some tea and made these cookies."

Carol said, "Hello, Shelley," in that same weary voice, and sat.

Inanely I said, "How are you, honey?"

"All right," she said automatically. The tone again belied the words, and so did everything else about her. Trouble dulled the gray-green of her eyes and gave her pretty mouth a down-at-the-corners appearance. A wisp of brown-blonde hair, out of place beneath the pert blue, white-ribboned straw hat, testified to her misery.

Mamie poured, said, "Drink this tea, darlin', while it's hot." She patted Carol on the shoulder and went back into the kitchen.

"Mr. Tinney'll be right down," I said, noting that it was three fifty-nine.

Don't believe this if you don't want to, but my saying that calmed her ever so slightly. Just his name. That's the kind of a man he was. People with troubles, who knew him, felt better just knowing he was going to step in.

She took a long puff on the cigarette and squashed it in the elephant tusk ash tray—the one Mr. Tinney claims was made from the tusks of a pachyderm he shot in the Belgian Congo. She lifted her cup to her lips and the tea spilled a little.

A door upstairs opened and closed softly and light, measured steps sounded. Carol looked up and I turned, and we watched him come down. He came very slowly, but not with the halting, uncertain slowness of the aged. You knew it wasn't that because he was straight as the light Malacca cane he carried, not for support, but merely as part of his wardrobe. I'd never seen him without it, indoors or out. And I'd never seen him lean on it. He didn't hold onto the banister, either.

You felt from the way he moved that he had simply decided there was no need to walk any faster.

Not that he wasn't an old man. He was. Very. His hair said so. It was white. Not silver or light gray, but white the way milk is white with just the faintest suggestion of a blue tint.

His face said he was a very old man, too. There were a lot of short, deep lines across his high forehead and on his cheeks. His skin looked very dry and you couldn't tell whether its tan-yellow color was the result of long years

beneath a blazing tropical sun or a plain lack of red cor-
puscles—or a little of both. He had the height and general
build of Lionel Barrymore. He occasionally remarked, as
a matter of fact, that Barrymore looked a little like him.

He reached the landing and his pale, sensitive lips
stretched into a warm smile. "Hello," he said, coming toward us, "I'm glad you came, Carol." He took the barrel-
backed chair between Carol's and mine.

"Mr. Tinney," the girl said, "the strangest thing has
happened. I don't know . . ."

"Excuse me, Carol," he said, "just one moment. Shelley, would you call Mamie, please?"

He wasn't playing the pampered master. He just never
raised his voice. His natural speaking tone was about three
degrees above a whisper, and it rarely varied. Not that it
wasn't expressive . . . it was.

He knew every trick of inflection and could get more
meaning into pauses of one kind and another than any
actor I've ever seen. I had a suspicion the reason he never
spoke loudly was that he was afraid the cracked quality of
his years would sneak out.

I opened my mouth to yell and closed it again because
Mamie walked in with the thing he'd wanted—a large
glassful of a thick, greenish liquid.

"Thank you, Mamie. Will you try some, Carol?"

The girl shook her head.

"Don't," I said, "it tastes like hell."

"I'll thank you to watch your language. Shelley," Mamie said. "Would you care for some more of my fine tea,
Carol?"

Carol said no thanks, and Mamie took the tray and
everything on it back into the kitchen.

Mr. Tinney chuckled after the broad six-foot three of
her and said to me, "Some day Mamie is going to spank
you."

"I've been worrying about that for years," I said.

Mr. Tinney sipped the greenish liquid—a juice squeezed from eight different vegetables—and half drank, half chewed it slowly. He set it down on the table and said, "Before you tell me about this strange thing that's happened, Carol, I want to confirm a thought I have . . . about Mr. Sikkim. Is it true that he—er, ah—made advances toward you himself?"

An expression of amazement and a little pain came into Carol's face. Mr. Tinney looked directly at her.

"I—I don't see . . . yes," she said, "yes, he did. How did you know?"

"I've been thinking about it for some time, Carol. He is so violently opposed to your marrying Ben that I felt I could safely eliminate all the obvious reasons for it, such as not wishing his son to marry a girl with less money or social position; wishing him to marry some other girl; any of a dozen other reasons. Then, too, if it were any of these orthodox reasons you would have told me what it was. The reason, therefore, can only be something very personal between you and Mr. Sikkim and something which you are reluctant to mention."

Mr. Tinney's blue eyes, wrinkle-squeezed so they were only as wide as a man's looking into a partly shaded lamp, shone. Any time he could display his analytical genius he was happy.

"Well," he said now, gesturing with his cane, "what, of such a nature, could have taken place between an employer and an employee? You are a very attractive girl, Carol, and I don't merely mean you have a pretty face. Your body, if you don't mind my saying so—well, even in that tailored suit your charms are hardly hidden."

The girl pinked, but she would have to do a lot more than that to stop Mr. Tinney now.

"So we have a dispute between a beautiful female employee and a male employer. The girl will not discuss this dispute even with her most trusted adviser. The situation becomes plain. Mr. Sikkim has made advances. You have forcibly rejected them. If he is a conceited man, as is certainly indicated by the fact that he wishes to rule a full-grown son's life, his fury will be unbounded. They say, 'Hell hath no fury like a woman scorned,' but I've found that the fury of a scorned lady is as nothing compared to that of an egotistical man who has been rebuffed." He leaned back in his chair, trying not to look too self-satisfied, and said, "Now, please, Carol, tell us what you started to say."

"Jimmy is back," she said abruptly. "I saw him day before yesterday—Monday. He was waiting in front of the house for me when I got home."

"That shouldn't disturb you, Carol. Your ties to Jimmy are completely severed."

"It's not just Jimmy," she said, "it's what happened. He looked so sad and . . . and poor and sick. He asked me to take him to dinner. I just couldn't refuse."

She lit another cigarette and puffed nervously. "We went to a little restaurant on Seventy-ninth Street and after dinner Jimmy asked to come up for just a few minutes to talk. He was so pitiful. He asked as though his life depended on it. So I took him up. And we talked for a little while and . . . and . . ."

She looked as though she didn't know what to say next. Mr. Tinney walked over to her and placed his hand on her shoulder.

"Don't be frightened, Carol," he said. "Just tell us what happened."

"That's just it," she said, "I don't know. We were talking and suddenly I began to feel very sleepy and that's all I remember until yesterday morning when I woke up in bed. I was in my pajamas, but I don't remember undressing or saying good-bye to Jimmy or . . . or anything at all."

"Have you searched your apartment? Is anything missing?" Mr. Tinney asked.

"Nothing," she said. "I thought maybe Jimmy had drugged me somehow during dinner. I did leave the table once just before dessert. I thought Jimmy might have taken my money, but it was right there in my purse. I only had four dollars and a little change, but it was all there. And I can't think of anything else I might have that Jimmy could possibly want."

"And what happened yesterday?" asked Mr. Tinney. How he knew anything had, I don't know.

"I got a telephone call," Carol said, "about noontime. A man called me. He wouldn't give his name, but he said if I would come to room 518 at the Hotel Wilkins at eleven-thirty last night he would tell me something of great importance to my future and to Ben's. He frightened me. I don't know why—his voice, the way he said the things he said, gave me the feeling he really knew something—something maybe that would explain Jimmy's returning or—or the way Mr. Sikkim feels about Ben and me."

"Did you go to the Wilkins?"

Carol nodded. "Yes. I asked at the desk who was registered in 518. The clerk wouldn't tell me. He said it was against their policy to give out the names of their guests. I stayed down in the lobby for ten or fifteen minutes, trying to make up my mind whether or not I ought to go up. Finally I did, but when I got to the door of 518 I lost my nerve. I tried to make myself knock, but I was so confused and frightened. I had the weirdest feeling that if I went into that room something terrible would happen. I finally left without seeing whoever had phoned me."

"And you haven't heard from him since?"

Carol shook her head.

"What makes you think all this had anything to do with Mr. Sikkim's attitude, Carol?" Mr. Tinney inquired.

"Ben told him Sunday that we were going to be married this week, whether he liked it or not. And he told Ben that he would stop the marriage if—if it was the last thing he did. I don't want to marry Ben under the circumstances, but I do, I honestly do, love him . . ." Her voice broke. "Ohhh, Mr. Tinney, I don't know what to do."

"I do, Carol," Mr. Tinney said. "You've objected to my seeing Mr. Sikkim ever since this situation arose. You insisted there was nothing anyone could do to change his mind. I'm going to see him today . . . right now. Do you mind?"

She shrugged her shoulders. "Maybe you can do something, Mr. Tinney. He'll still be in the office, I believe. Mr. Kerwin gave me the afternoon off, but Mr. Sikkim was still there when I left."

Mr. Tinney saw Carol to the door, came backhand said, "Get me the address please, Shelley."

I went to the file where we had the names, addresses and phone numbers of all our clients, and everyone they were mixed up with, and saw that Siquin, Inc., was on Fifth Avenue between Fifty-sixth and Fifty-seventh Streets. "Okay," I said, "let's go."

Desmond Tinney's home and office is a two-story whitestone on West Ninety-third Street, just off Central Park, and as I drove west to Columbus Avenue I started to tell him about Wakely again.

But he had a new problem to play with and I should have known better. He talked about Sikkim and Carol Wills. I kept talking about Wakely and the program. It developed into a lovely but pointless conversation which ended when I pulled up in front of Siquin's.

It was a four-story building that looked as though it had been scrubbed yesterday. A plate glass window was its entire first floor front except for the door to the building, which was on the left. In the window there was one of those smart, restrained displays for *Morning's Laughter by Siquin*. The display was built around an original oil painting of a black-haired, blue-eyed beauty as Irish as the Blarney Stone. Her open mouth and the sparkle in her eyes were so real you could almost hear the sound of her laughter.

"Stop gaping, Shelley," Mr. Tinney said, leading the way into the building, "It's only a picture."

On the fourth floor we walked past a reception desk, the guardian of which was probably out powdering her nose; then through a door and down a short corridor, office-lined on both sides. At the end of the corridor was a door with the name *Amerandra Sikkim* on it.

Mr. Tinney stopped two feet from the door and raised the cane in his right hand to halt me. He walked forward cautiously and bent over, his head cocked in a listening attitude. As I reached his side, I heard the voice, too. It was high-pitched and the words spurted like sparks from a live wire.

"I've waited and waited, and I intended to wait a little longer, but you've forced my hand . . ."

Mr. Tinney looked around and frowned at me and said sharply, "Shelley!" as though the eavesdropping had been my idea. He rapped politely with his cane.

The voice stopped, and there was a moment when the silence seemed to be crashing against the door from the inside, trying to get out.

Then a bass voice, a little shaky, said, "Come in."

Mr. Tinney opened the door and I followed him in. We were almost bowled over by a tall, thin, Latin-looking guy, about my own age, thirty, who came storming out. He was so mad he was actually snorting. His skin was a pale yellow and his dark brown eyes shot flame back at the man at the desk. The door quivered on its hinges as he slammed it behind him.

Amerandra Sikkim looked like a man who hadn't slept in a month. His murky black eyes were bloodshot. There was a nervous twitch at the right corner of his thin lips and his cheeks were sucked in so the lines of teeth on either side showed against the purplish-tan skin, peculiar to the people of India.

He managed a smile and, in a peculiar Oxford accent, said, "That was Frangipanni, my chief perfumer. Ranting on about a bonus I was supposed to have promised him. Now, what may I do for you, gentlemen?"

Mr. Tinney did the introductions, indicating no surprise at all at Sikkim's nervous appearance. We took chairs on either side of the desk.

"I'm in a very peculiar business, Mr. Sikkim," he said. "The business of minding other people's business."

"You've probably heard Mr. Tinney on the air," I inserted. "We broadcast for Wakely's Soapchips every Tuesday night."

"Never mind the advertising, Shelley," Mr. Tinney said sharply. "Mr. Sikkim, your son's happiness must mean a great deal to you."

Sikkim took a cigar out of a humidor on his desk, passed it to Mr. Tinney and me with no results, and said, "It does, Mr. Tinney, naturally. But I want to save your time and mine. If you are going to try to convince me that I should sanction my son's marriage to that Wills girl, I refuse to listen. I do not know how long you've known the girl, but I have known her for two years, and she is not the kind of girl I want my son to marry. That is final."

"Would you mind telling me, honestly and frankly, why?" asked Mr. Tinney politely.

The telephone on Sikkim's desk rang. Picking it up, he said, "Excuse me," then into the mouthpiece, "Hello. Yes . . . she what? See here, Benabala, I've warned you all along about that girl. . . . No . . ."

A crackling that somehow conveyed hysteria sounded, in the ear piece, even across to where Mr. Tinney and I were sitting. I noticed the look of alarm in Mr. Tinney's eyes and then Sikkim screamed, "No! I will not! They can hang her for all I care!" And he slammed the phone back into its cradle.

He turned to Mr. Tinney and said very deliberately, "Miss Wills has just been picked up on suspicion of murder. She is being held in the Women's House of Detention until such time as someone will furnish ten thousand dollars bail for her. My son just phoned to ask me to put up the ten thousand dollars. I, as you may have gathered, refused. Good day, gentlemen."

2

The thing that got us the Wakely program, our first air show, was the stunt I pulled when practically one cop out of every three seemed to be committing suicide. The commissioner was half, crazy trying to find an answer to it. He'd tried psychiatrists and psychologists and psychoanalysts and psychoeverything elses. But the police suicide tolls kept mounting. Seventy cops, you'll recall, did the dutch last May alone. I offered the commissioner Desmond Tinney, the man who'd solved more personal problems of all kinds, than any other fifteen so-called human relations counselors all put together. It was a last straw and the commissioner grabbed it.

At the time, I'd kept my fingers crossed, wondering whether Mr. Tinney would be able to do anything. He did. He put on a show. Every cop on the force was officially requested to attend. The Garden was jammed. And then he paraded out the wives and the kids, the fathers and mothers, the sisters and brothers of the cops who'd knocked themselves off. They all made speeches about what the suicide of their cop had done to them. It was the most brutal, heart-tearing, blood-curdling demonstration I've ever seen. It would have brought tears to Himmler's eyes! But it stopped police suicides—cold! There hasn't been one in the last eight months, and I doubt if there will ever be one as long as the memory of that demonstration lasts.

That made Mr. Tinney the number one human relations counselor in the city, and, for my money, in the world. But it did something else that was going to come in handy now. It made him the fair-haired boy of the force. He was an honorary captain, had a badge to prove it, and every cop in town, from the highest to the lowest, swore by him. So far I'd gotten six tickets fixed on the strength of it, and now that it seemed Mr. Tinney was going to stick his nose into a murder investigation, I could see how it wouldn't hurt at all.

And he *was* going to stick his nose into it.

"Drive down to the Women's House of, Detention, Shelley," he said. "In all my years of attempting to aid people in trouble, I've never run into a single murder case. I've often wondered how I would fare if faced with a problem of that kind."

"I might remind you," I said, "that you have very little time to play detective. There's the little matter of a weekly one-hour radio show. Wakely and Catlett and Hall, the agency, are plenty peeved because you didn't let the announcer work in the closing commercial last night."

"Now listen, Shelley. You know I couldn't. I wasn't finished with that poor Timmins woman. And I refuse to hurry those unfortunate people just to let some fool announcer bleat about soap chips."

"That bleating is what you get fifteen hundred dollars a week for," I reminded him.

"Yes, and it's also what forces me to put the people who come to me on display like a bunch of freaks. I'm getting sick and . . ."

"Now wait, Mr. Tinney; you know you're doing a lot more good than you've ever been able to do before, just because you're on the air. Think of the millions of people who can benefit from your broadcast!"

"You've told me all that before, Shelley."

I changed the subject. "I talked to that publisher again," I said. "He's willing to raise the ante on the advance for that book of your outstanding cases to five hundred dollars . . ."

"Shelley! I've told you a thousand times, I absolutely will not write a book about people's troubles."

I was going to say I'd write it—I might even be able to work in some of my own original poems—but I'd said that before, too. I was also going to bring up the subject of the Wakely agency's order that from now on the program be rehearsed and they see the running script before we go on. I thought better of it, and we were pulling up at the Women's Detention House anyway.

Captain Henry Frieze had taken over. He came down the short hall from the cell block with the cop who'd been sent in to tell him we were there.

"Hello, Mr. Tinney," he said in his cold, flat voice.

"Hello, Hank. You remember Stanley Shell. Hank, I'm interested in that Wills girl. I understand she's being held on suspicion of homicide."

Captain Frieze nodded his pale bald head. The frigid blue of his eyes showed nothing as he said, "I've just been talking to her. It doesn't look good."

He led the way down the corridor into the cell block.

A frowzy, yellow-headed dame in one of the cells yelled, "Hey, Captain, how about a little drinkee?" as we passed. Two cells further down, on the opposite side, Carol Wills sat on a leather-covered cot with a frightened look in her eyes. A little of the fright went out of them when she saw Mr. Tinney.

He said, "Hello, Carol. Where's Ben?"

"If you mean that young madman who was here with her," Frieze said, "he's gone out to raise ten grand."

A young guy stood in the far corner of the cell. He walked toward us and Frieze said, "John, this is Mr. Tinney and Stanley Shell. . . . John Ryan from the DA.'s office."

"Oh, yes," Ryan said with a grin I didn't like, "you're the gent who saved the police department."

"You know anything about this at all, Mr. Tinney?" Frieze asked.

"Nothing."

"Well, if you're going to help"—I was more amazed than ever that even a hard-boiled cop like Frieze took it for granted Mr. Tinney could help—"if you're going to help, I'd better bring you up to date on it. Or would you rather tell it, Miss Wills?"

Carol shook her head dumbly.

Frieze said, "Barney Stark, one of the house dicks at the Hotel Wilkins, called us this morning about ten o'clock. The chambermaid found a guy stabbed to death in room 518."

I didn't want to, but I stared at Carol. That was the room she'd been hovering around last night. Now she just stared miserably ahead of her.

And Frieze was going on with his story. "Schultz and Beavins and me went over there. The dead guy turned out to be Noel Landry. He was a private shamus that everyone called 'Angles,' and not for nothing. He had a reputation for working every job he got fifty-six ways to the middle, the middle being little Noel. He wasn't only stabbed. The knife had been stuck in him and ripped right down his middle.

"We didn't find the shiv that was used to kill him, but we found a little tin box hidden in one of the bureau drawers." He turned to the assistant district attorney. "John, you got that stuff?"

Ryan reached into the inside pocket of his neat Oxford blue double-breasted, pulled out several envelopes, and handed them to Frieze. Frieze took a photograph out of one and I noticed deep crimson climb right up to Carol Wills' cheeks, as she hung her head.

"We found a few items," Frieze said. "This picture, for instance." He handed it to Mr. Tinney.

I looked over his shoulder at it and I think I blushed too. It showed Carol in a badly mussed-up bed in the arms of Jimmy Knight. It was a side view and Carol's right arm was around Jimmy's neck, her eyes closed, which seemed quite appropriate for such a moment.

"See that newspaper on the chair alongside the bed there?" said Frieze.

Mr. Tinney said, "Yes," and I nodded.

Frieze said, "We made an enlargement." He handed Mr. Tinney another photo, just a blown-up section of the newspaper on the chair. "You can see the date on the paper plain as day, 'Monday, October 13.' That was just day before yesterday."

Again Mr. Tinney nodded.

Frieze took another item from one of the other envelopes. "Here's a list," he said, handing a sheet of yellow paper to Mr. Tinney, "of what seems to be every perfume manufacturer in town and the name 'O'Hara.'"

From what I could see of the list, it seemed to contain some sixteen or seventeen names and addresses. Scrawled in pencil at the bottom of the typewritten list was the single word "O'Hara."

"And this," said Frieze, "is the wackiest part of the whole setup."

He took a small buff-colored sheet of linen stationery out of an envelope and as he handed it to Mr. Tinney a peculiar fragrance hit my nostrils. My first olfactory impression was that it smelled offensive, but then, as it came closer, a strange change seemed to take place to my nostrils. The offensiveness disappeared entirely and the oddest blend of definitely pleasant aromas reached me.

Mr. Tinney sniffed at the paper and said, "Mmm. This is a strange perfume."

"Read the note," Frieze said. "That's even stranger."

In typewritten capital letters, it said:

THE ODOR OF LOVE HAS TURNED TO HATE. LEST IT LINGER NO LONGER IN YOUR NOSTRILS—THIS REMINDER.

Instead of a signature, there was a black ink sketch of a lot of slanted lines with small, shaky ovals and circles over them.

"There were two of them," Frieze said, as we stared at the first note. "Here's the other."

The paper, typing, signature and odor were exactly alike. This one said:

BREATHE DEEPLY OF THE ODOR YOU KNEW SO WELL—FOR SOON YOU WILL BREATHE NO MORE.

"Here's one other thing we found," said Frieze. "I can't make anything out of it, but it may be important."

He lifted the flap of a smaller envelope, held it topside down, and shook a piece of reddish rubber into his hand. It was about two inches long and maybe an eighth of an inch square.

Mr. Tinney took it, studied it for a moment, then handed it back without comment. Frieze replaced the various items in their envelopes and handed them over to the assistant D. A.

"It wasn't any trouble at all picking up Miss Wills," Frieze explained. "Within five minutes after we got on the case we had the whole department out with dupes of the photo, checking the names on the list and the people over at the hotel. The guy on the desk last night and the elevator guy who ran her up told us the girl in the picture had been there, just before midnight. Doc Kammerer, the medical examiner, told us that Landry had been killed just about that time.

"We found a hackie who drove her home from the Wilkins last night and he remembered her and took us right to where she lived on Seventy-ninth Street. We had a couple of men waiting there when she showed up about an hour ago and they brought her right down here."

He looked down at Carol, sitting forlornly on the cot, and said, "Would you like to tell Mr. Tinney everything you told us, Miss Wills?"

Carol answered dully, "No, he knows everything there is to know."

Frieze continued, "She told us about this guy in the picture being a slug she'd married and about how the marriage was annulled and how this guy came to see her day before yesterday . . . and about this Ben Sikkim she's figuring on marrying now and his old man and . . ."

"She told you she was at the Wilkins last night and about the phone call, didn't she?" asked Mr. Tinney.

Frieze nodded.

Ryan busted in finally with, "Look, Tinney . . ."

Mr. Tinney scowled at him and said, *Mister* Tinney, please!"

"All right, Mr. Tinney. Look, if you want to help this kid, will you, for God's sake, tell her it'll go easier on her if she confesses instead of stalling around? After all, it's open and shut. She went to the Wilkins, went up to 518—

we can prove that—and Landry showed her this picture and threatened to show it to her boy friend, so she stabbed him. It's blackmail, there's no question about that. Juries go comparatively easy on blackmail killings, but let's cut the comedy; let's sew the thing up."

Mr. Tinney turned to Carol Wills. He said quietly, "Did you kill Landry, Carol?"

The girl shook her head dumbly. "No," she said, "no. I never saw him in my life."

"There you are, Mr. Ryan," said Mr. Tinney.

Ryan's face reddened. He waved his arms wildly. "There I am!" he screamed. "There I am! For crisakes, what do you expect her to say? I'm telling you it's open and . . ."

"All right, John," Frieze said, "take it easy. There's no rush."

"What?" exploded Ryan again. "No rush? What kind of cop are you? You're supposed to solve cases, not make them tougher by pampering the prisoner."

"Pampering, nuts! If Miss Wills did it, she'll tell us sooner or later. If she didn't do it, we want to get after whoever did as soon as possible."

"A fine thing! A fine thing!" stormed Ryan. "But I'm telling you right now I'm filing a murder charge this afternoon." He went to the door and yelled for the turn-key.

"Don't pay any attention to him," Frieze said. "He's hungry for convictions. He wants to cinch his job as chief assistant."

"If he files the charge you won't be able to release Miss Wills on bail, will you?" asked Mr. Tinney.

"No," said Frieze.

"Well, come on then. Let's get busy and find out who really killed Mr. Landry." Mr. Tinney turned to Carol, patted her gently on the shoulder and said, "Don't worry, Carol. We'll have you out of here very soon."

I thought I saw the faintest flicker of a grin on Frieze's face as he moved toward the cell door. We followed him out and to one of the offices on the lower floor in the front of the building.

"What about Ben?" Mr. Tinney asked, when we had settled down in chairs.

"As far as I'm concerned," answered Frieze, "we've got as good a case against him as we have against the girl. He was waiting at Miss Wills' house for her when the boys picked her up and they brought him right along. I asked him where he was last night around eleven-thirty to midnight and he didn't know. He said he'd had an argument about ten o'clock with his old man about the girl and he'd walked out in a huff and got in his car and drove and drove and drove until about three this morning. He don't know where he drove or why. He just drove. He's a pretty high-strung and nervous boy, and if he found out about that picture and Landry I can see him knocking 'Angles' off a lot quicker than I can see that girl doing it."

"I'm inclined to agree with you," said Mr. Tinney. "What did Miss Wills say about the perfumed notes and the list of manufacturers?"

"Nothing. She said she didn't know a thing about either of them."

"What do you make of them, Hank?"

Frieze shrugged his thin shoulders. "Probably a case Landry was working on for somebody. I can't see him getting the kind of kill warning in those notes. That list and those notes are the reason I'm not in too much of a hurry to throw the book at that kid. I'd like to know a lot more about them before I make up my mind about who killed 'Angles.'

"There are probably a couple of dozen citizens around who wouldn't mind cutting him up a little. The last five of six years he's steered clear of the racket boys—they're too nasty to play with the way Landry played—but we've had reports from a couple of stoolies already that 'Angles' was around asking after some of the boys in the old liquor mobs."

"What about that 'O'Hara' he scribbled on the bottom of that list?" I put in.

Again Frieze shrugged. "There's a private dick by that name, Jeff O'Hara. Another fastie. I'm figuring on talking to him as soon as the boys pick him up."

Mr. Tinney stood up. "Have you talked to Mr. Sikkim yet, Hank?"

"No. I was going to. Do you know him?"

"I met him today for the first time. A very interesting gentleman. If you're going to talk to him, Shelley and I would like to go along."

My watch said it was four minutes past six—just a little over two hours since Carol had come to Mr. Tinney's home.

"Got a phone book, Hank?" I asked. "I'll call Sikkim's office to see if he's still there."

He wasn't. An unhappy female voice at Siquin's told me he'd left to keep an appointment and was then going home. I looked up his home number in Great Neck, called and learned he was expected in about an hour.

"Let's go," Frieze said. "If he's a little late, we'll wait."

Out on the street we decided to use Frieze's police car. I was going to pick ours up later. Frieze went around to the left side of the car to get in behind the steering wheel. He'd just opened the door when I saw an arm grab him and whirl him around. I started to squeeze out behind the wheel when I heard a hysterical voice that sounded familiar.

"Captain! I'm glad I found you. I want to confess. I killed Landry."

I got out and it was Ben Sikkim all right, wilder looking than I'd ever seen him. People stopped on the street and stared and gaped as he kept yelling that he'd killed Landry, until finally Frieze got him by the arm and yanked him across the sidewalk and into the jail building.

"For crisakes," he said sharply, as we reached the door, "you're certainly seeing to it you confess with enough witnesses around."

Mr. Tinney caught up as we took seats around a desk in the same office we'd left.

Frieze picked up the phone. "Frieze talking," he said, "in office D. Send in a stenographer."

"Knew she'd gone out with him," Ben started to rave. "I followed them all night. I saw them go into the hotel. I . . . I . . ."

"Wait a minute," Frieze said.

"What did you do with the ice pick?" Mr. Tinney asked.

"I took it along," Ben said. "I walked over to the North River. I threw it in. I couldn't stand the idea of him—"

"Was it the kind of wound that could have been made with an ice pick, Hank?"

"Hell no," Frieze sighed, reaching for the phone. "Frieze again," he said into it. "Cancel the stenographer."

Mr. Tinney was standing over Ben, talking quietly to him. "It doesn't matter if you weren't able to get the bail, Ben. I've already arranged for it. Carol will be out of here in less than an hour."

This was news to me, especially since we had less than four thousand dollars in the bank.

"Where," I asked Mr. Tinney on the way to the car, "are you going to get ten thousand dollars? And besides, Ryan is filing the murder charge and you won't be able to bail her out."

"Shelley, you do as I tell you now. I'll have no arguments about it. If we get the bond money before the charge is filed, I believe they'll have to release her. I'm going out to Sikkim's with Captain Frieze alone. I want you to get

Ben to a doctor. I don't care how you do it, as long as you do. If something isn't done for that boy right away, he'll have a nervous breakdown."

"But—"

"And before you do that I want you to post the bond for Miss Wills."

"Where do I get it?"

"Call up Wakely and tell him to advance it. Tell him we'll quit if he doesn't."

"You can't quit. There's a contract."

"Just tell him that," said Mr. Tinney, and joined Frieze in the car.

I could see Frieze asking about young Sikkim and Mr. Tinney explaining; then Frieze drove off and I was left standing there on the sidewalk with Ben tugging at my sleeve and asking excitedly, "Was that true what he said about Carol's bail?"

"Sure. I've got to make a phone call, that's all."

3

If you think I got the ten thousand, you're crazier than Mr. Tinney. I was working from behind the eight ball to begin with, because Wakely, whose home phone number I had, assumed I was going to tell him Mr. Tinney had okayed the idea of turning in a pre-broadcast script and rehearsing the show. When I hemmed and hawed up to the point where I told him no, the boss hadn't attended to those little details yet, but how about ten thousand dollars in advance, he nearly shattered my eardrum with his bellow.

What could I say then except, "Ha, ha . . . can't you take a joke, Mr. Wakely? I just thought—"

"A joke?" he roared. "You take me away from my dinner to ask me a thing like that, and then you call it a joke! Listen, Shell, we've put up with a lot of insanity from Mr. Tinney because the show's Crosley rating has been pretty high. But even if he tops Bob Hope, we won't stand for any displays of lunacy from you. One madman is enough. And you'd better bring in that script and let me know about the rehearsals—or else!"

Somehow my eardrum withstood the second assault, that of the phone on the other end being hung up.

I came out of the drugstore booth really worried. I wanted to help Carol Wills as much as possible, and I knew that Mr. Tinney hadn't been fooling about wanting me to

get the ten thousand dollars. I didn't see how I could even
make a serious try at getting it without risking losing the
show. Mr. Tinney, I knew, didn't give a damn whether we
lost it and the fifteen hundred a week that went with it.
But I'll admit I did. I was with Mr. Tinney for five years
before we got the show, and I'd stay with him if we lost
it, but believe me, it wasn't fun. While Mr. Tinney seemed
to be perfectly contented as long as he had his vegetable
juice, Bing Crosby, his cane, and a flock of people running to him with their troubles, I prefer a slightly fuller
personal life. Like eating three times a day, going out with
a nice girl to a nice place, buying books of poetry, and a
few other things.

I didn't have much time to figure out what to do next,
though, because Ben Sikkim grabbed me as soon as I
stepped out of the booth.

"Isn't it all right?" he asked frantically, having guessed
from my face, I suppose, that it wasn't.

"Yeah, sure it's all right," I said. "Come on with me
now. We're going to have a doctor give you a little shot of
something to soothe your nerves."

"No," he objected, "I'm going back to the—the prison.
I want to wait until Carol gets out."

I probably should have led up to it more diplomatical-
ly, maybe told him we were going to get the ten thousand
and then sneak him into a doctor's, but I wasn't thinking
about Ben's nerves too much. Aside from wanting to get
back to Mr. Tinney to get his ideas about straightening
out Wakely and maybe still getting the money, I wanted
to get in on at least part of the session with Frieze, Mr.
Tinney and Sikkim, Senior. A guy like me doesn't run into
a murder case every day in his life and I wanted to see how
this one would work out.

"Look, Ben, we're going to a doctor," I said.

"No, we're not. I'm not, anyway. I'm staying right with Carol until—"

I pointed to the door and said, "Why, there's Carol now."

He turned his head and I swung my right from way back and way down. My aim was good. Pain shot up my arm and I thought I'd broken his neck when my fist crashed against the side of his jaw. And then, as his head hit the edge of the phone booth on the way to the floor, I thought he'd fractured his skull. I knelt beside him and felt his pulse. I listened to his heart beat and it sounded all right.

The druggist came rushing out from behind his counter, saying nervously, "What's the matter? Why are you fighting?"

"We're not fighting. My friend was a little drunk and didn't want to go home. His wife is worried sick about him. I've got to get him home right away."

I managed to get Ben up and over my shoulder and staggered out and down the street to the car with him. I tossed him in the front seat, got in myself, and started uptown, fully intending to take him to Doc Schwartz on Ninety-ninth Street. When we got up to Fifty-seventh, though, he was still slumbering so peacefully, I thought, "Hell, a good rest is all he needs and he's getting that, so I'll just drive him home and put him to bed."

I swung left and onto Queensborough Bridge, and headed for Great Neck.

Ben was still sound asleep when I turned through the gates into the private road leading up to the Sikkim house. The private road seemed almost as long as the drive out from New York. And the grounds on either side of it looked like generous chunks of some of our better-kept city parks. There were as many and as pretty trees, but the grass seemed to have been cut more carefully. When I got closer to the place itself I saw that calling it a house was a little like calling the Atlantic Ocean a puddle. Even *mansion* would have been gross understatement. Knowing practically nothing about architecture, I would have said it was Georgian. At least it had long white pillars and arches and things.

I skipped the garages, which were off toward the rear and the left, and swung right and pulled up in front of the house itself. Dragging Ben out of the car and getting him onto my shoulder, I noticed far off to the right a bunch of gay-striped cabanas, standing in line like headless toy soldiers, and, in front of the cabanas, a swimming pool that a small yacht could probably cruise around in..

"Maybe," I thought, "I ought to muscle into the perfume business."

I was halfway up the broad white steps when the huge door opened and a guy who looked like a long-retired bank president, but turned out to be a butler, came down to meet me.

"Is that Master Ben you have there? Is something wrong?" he asked anxiously.

"It's him," I flaunted the grammatical codes, "but there's nothing wrong. He's asleep."

"Please, sir, let me take him."

I frowned at the old boy, doubting whether he could hold Ben up, but he slid him from my shoulder to his own and stood almost as erect as before.

"If you'll pardon my asking, sir, would you mind not saying anything about bringing Master Ben home?"

"Why not? Isn't he supposed to come home?"

"Yes, but Mrs. Sikkim would worry. He hasn't been well lately and if I just get him up to bed and . . ."

"Sure," I said, "go ahead. Where's the party?"

"In the library, sir. Straight ahead and around to your right."

"Thanks."

He walked off to the left, then turned left again.

For maybe three minutes I thought I'd gotten myself lost. I walked through rooms that looked like museums I'd been in. High-ceilinged, with ornate, rococo-framed oil paintings of people who were undoubtedly somebody's ancestors; chairs, tables and couches that looked like they had been passed down through many generations and would be passed down through many more. The clue I finally got was the voices. I followed them and reached the door of a room that looked like six or seven Union League clubs rolled into one. I stood there and watched and listened to Sikkim, Senior, battle with a tall, broad-shouldered man with iron-gray hair.

"I will not advance a single cent of the firm's capital to post bond for that girl, Randolph," Sikkim was saying in a strained voice. Agitation showed, too, in the perceptible quivering of his hands, the pallor around his mouth, and the flare of his nostrils.

"You've done a lot of things, Amer," the tall man said between clamped teeth, "that have made me ashamed to be associated with you, but this tops them all. You know that girl—"

"I will not stand for your insinuations," Sikkim roared.

But Captain Frieze got up out of the maroon leather armchair in which he'd been seated.

"Gentlemen," he said, "if you don't mind, I'd appreciate it if you'd settle this matter of the bond later. We've waited close to an hour for Mr. Sikkim to arrive, and now that he's here I'd like to ask him a few questions that might help this investigation."

The tall man nodded curtly and moved back to stand beside a slim woman with almost snow-white hair and fine, chiseled features in a face that had a peculiar old-young look. She sat huddled in a corner of a huge chair.

Sikkim walked to a couch and sat down beside a dainty-looking fashion plate with rimless glasses. He was dainty-looking except for a thick, hairbrush mustache, and a fashion plate except for his shirt. It seemed much too large for him. There was plenty of space between the inside of its collar and his neck, and the cuffs were loose and floppy. Maybe a new style, I thought.

Mr. Tinney was seated over near one corner of the room, with his cane between his legs. I could tell by the stiffness with which he sat in the chair he was Observing—and I mean with a capital "O."

I cleared my throat and all eyes turned toward me.

"Pardon me," Mr. Tinney said, "but I would like to present Stanley Shell, my personal manager."

I came in and Frieze did the introductions, fast and neat. The fashion plate with the large shirt and the mustache was Francis Roche; the tall guy who'd been battling Sikkim was Randolph Kerwin, Carol Wills' boss and Sikkim's partner; the lady huddled in the chair, Mrs. Amerandra Sikkim. Then the fun began.

"I'll make this as fast as possible, Mr. Sikkim," Frieze said. "We found several peculiar notes, doused with a perfume we've been unable to identify, in Noel Landry's coat pocket. In the same pocket we also found a list of all the perfume manufacturers in the city. It's natural for us to guess the notes were sent to someone and that that someone turned them over to Landry for investigation. The notes threatened death."

"I know nothing of any notes," Sikkim said, "but if you care to have me examine them, I may be able to identify the odor. For that matter, Mr. Kerwin or Mr. Roche may be able to identify the odor. All three of us are more or less expert perfumers."

"You in the perfume business, too, Mr. Roche?" Frieze asked the dapper man.

"I was a perfumer-chemist. I formerly owned a chain of exclusive perfume shops. I have lectured on all phases of perfumery, and still do for that matter. And I am now executive secretary of the Allied Perfumers' Association." His mustache moved up over a smile as he finished, "I do know a little about perfumes. And I'll be happy to be of service."

"Thanks," Frieze said, and took out the envelope with the notes. "Maybe one of you gentlemen can tell me something about this smell."

They took the notes and sniffed. There was something about the way each of them sniffed that stamped them as professionals, even though their technique differed. Sikkim held the notes about four inches away from his nose and seemed to inhale slowly. Then he dropped the note to his side and held his breath. He didn't move a muscle in his face. For a minute he stood perfectly still.

Then he said, "It's an odor which I have never encountered before. A very peculiar odor. There are features of it which would lead one to say it is a distinctly Oriental type and yet it carries a characteristic of softness which finds no place in the heavier, Oriental perfumes—a decidedly unusual odor."

Sikkim didn't even bother to read the notes. Kerwin did and spent less time than did Sikkim with the smell test. He admitted he was stumped, too, and said Sikkim had described the perfume quite accurately. Roche dawdled over the business longer than either of the other two, but he wound up with the same answer Sikkim had given us, though in slightly different language.

"It seems to me," he concluded, "that the dominating odor note might be ylang ylang, but as Mr. Sikkim says, a certain subtleness of the odor seems to contradict that. I believe chemical analysis by a perfumer-chemist will be necessary to properly identify it."

"What's ylang ylang?" asked Frieze.

"It is an oil that is distilled from the flowers of the ylang ylang tree, cultivated mainly in Manila, although there are sections of Java and Reunion where the trees are grown."

"Yeah, I see," said Frieze. "Let's leave it lay."

Sikkim looked at his watch and said with sudden impatience, "Captain, please hasten this pointless investigation. I can tell you just one thing about Mr. Landry and I will proceed to tell you that without hesitation. I hired Mr. Landry to investigate and discover for me, if possible, the head of a ring which has been hurting my business considerably. This ring has been making counterfeit bottles and labels of the leading and most expensive brands of perfumes. Siquin's is naturally included. In certain stores, the agents of this ring are able to persuade dishonest buyers to purchase the counterfeit perfumes at prices which are naturally far below our regularly established prices. Customers purchase the perfumes and consequently are greatly disappointed in the quality of the merchandise. From that time on they are lost to us as customers."

"Isn't the storekeeper cutting his own throat by making dissatisfied customers?" Frieze asked.

"Certainly, Captain," Roche took up the explanation, "but, in a tremendous number of cases, the man who buys the perfumes is not actually the owner of the store. He is merely the soap and perfume or the drug buyer. He, therefore, is able to pocket a sizable amount of money over and above his regular salary and commissions. And this counterfeit ring is thus able to stay in business."

"It's a lot like the racket some of the old alky boys took up after prohibition was repealed," Frieze said. "They used to counterfeit labels and bottles of standard brand liquors, fill them with hogwash, and sell them to retailers. This racket's been reported to the police, hasn't it?"

"Of course, Captain," Roche said again. "I've had numerous consultations with Inspector Healy as well as with a number of your detectives. They have arrested several minor personages in the ring—salesmen, agents, and persons of that type—but the practice continues to flourish. It is an evil with which the association has been trying to cope for some time."

"How come you hired a private operator to handle this for you, Mr. Sikkim?" Frieze asked. "Ain't the cops good enough for you?"

"Obviously not, Captain," Sikkim said angrily. "Mr. Roche has just explained to you that the city police have accomplished nothing. Mr. Roche acted for the association, but I must protect my own business. If I feel a private detective agency can help me, I have every right to employ one."

"You're right," Frieze said placatingly. "Did Landry er—ah—accomplish anything?"

"He did not, but yesterday, which was the last time I saw him, he came to my office and told me he expected to have some important news for me very soon. It is entirely possible that he was murdered by a person who might be involved by the information Landry intended to pass on to me. That is as much as I can tell you. And now, if you'll excuse me, Mr. Roche and I have some very important matters to discuss."

"Wait a minute, Amer," Randolph Kerwin said. "For the last time, are you going to countersign this check I've made out for ten thousand dollars?"

"Curse you, Randolph! For the last time, no! Miss Wills is a cheap, common tramp and it wouldn't surprise me in the least to learn that she actually did murder Mr. Landry. She can—"

I don't know whether we looked before or after the sound. I had the weird impression that there was flame

in the doorway, as though the heavy drapes had caught
fire. And then came the sound—a low, animal sound, half
growl and half cry, and I looked toward the entrance to
the room and saw Ben Sikkim standing there. He was the
closest thing to a lunatic I have ever seen. His black hair
was in wild disarray, his shirt was open at the throat, and
his tie was awry. His pants were soggy-looking and wrink-
led. His tanned face was shiny with sweat, and the shine
burned in his eyes and melted in slobber at the corner of
his lips. His hands were as wet as his face and they hung
and quivered at his sides as though they were electrified.

He made the sound in his throat and walked with odd,
jerking steps across the room toward his father.

Mrs. Sikkim cried, "Darling!" in an anguished mother-
voice.

Mr. Tinney said with quiet insistence, "Ben, I want to
talk to you."

Kerwin barked, "Ben, don't . . ."

None of it did any good. Ben came on.

He was two feet from his father when Frieze stepped
in front of him, grabbed both his arms, and said, "Take it
easy, kid, take it easy."

And Amerandra Sikkim said in a hard, merciless voice,
"Take your hands off him, Captain. Let him come."

Frieze must have felt the same thing we all did—that this
was between father and son and must be faced. He stepped
aside. Ben advanced and his tortured eyes blazed into his
father's clouded brown ones. Words ripped out of his throat.

"Take that . . . back . . . Father!"

The left corner of Amerandra Sikkim's lip lifted in a
sneer, which screamed, Fool! Fool! Fool! louder than if
he'd used his voice.

Ben's right hand came up like an automaton's and
slapped hard across his father's left cheek. A trickle of
blood showed at the corner of the lip, and the fingers

and hand marks were buff against the purplish-brown of Amerandra Sikkim's face.

"Aaa . . . aapologize . . ." Ben spluttered.

Just for one fleeting second the hardness melted out of Amerandra Sikkim's face. Everything about it, the eyes, the mouth, the set of the jaw, softened and his voice softened, too. He was a man transformed. Almost tenderly he said, "Son, you are ill. Go to your room."

Ben's hand rose and fell in another stiff slap on his father's face and all the softness went out of it quicker than it had come. Amerandra's arm raised and swept down in a vicious arc and smashed against the side of Ben's head. Ben's knees buckled but he screamed and leaped at his father and his fingers found his father's throat.

"Take it back before I kill you . . . take it back . . . take it back or I'll kill you . . ."

The words came fast now, and scratchy, as though his gritted teeth slashed them as they passed through.

Frieze and Kerwin and Roche and I all rushed in to try to tear Ben's hands from his father's throat. And it took the four of us, the distinguished-looking butler, who had appeared from nowhere, and Mrs. Sikkim, who was trying to squeeze through, to do it. At that we hardly did it in time. The purplish hue of Amerandra Sikkim's face had deepened alarmingly and the marks of Ben's thumbs were like two white holes in his throat. He gasped and coughed as he staggered back into a chair.

Frieze, Kerwin, Roche, the butler and I held Ben's savagely struggling arms and shoulders and his mother got in front of him. Tears were in her eyes, but not in her voice.

"Ben, darling . . . Ben . . . Ben . . ." she kept saying over and over, in soothing, half cooing tones.

It was no good. Ben kept kicking and squirming until he suddenly went all limp in our hands. Then he straightened and raised his head and laughed and kept right on

laughing, as though somebody had just told him the fun-
niest story of the year. Usually uproarious laughter makes
everybody else around laugh, too. But this laughter didn't.
It made you feel like someone was shooting dice with ice
cubes all along your spine.

The laughter reached its highest pitch and Ben kept
stiffening; then it went back down the scale and Ben went
gradually limp with it till he passed out cold. I wished I'd
taken him to the Doc's.

I looked over to where Mr. Tinney was sitting. He
looked as if he hadn't moved an inch all through this
crisis. He was still sitting straight up in the chair, and his
blue eyes stared at us with hardly a blink.

Mrs. Sikkim said, "Please, get him upstairs to his room."

I looked toward her. I'd been standing at Ben's right
and slightly behind him and she'd been standing in front
of him. She moved now to lead the way to the door and
I noticed for the first time she had no right arm, just an
empty sleeve tucked into the belt of her dress.

4

"You were a big help all through that," I told Mr. Tinney when we were in the car again on our way back to New York.

He didn't even get angry. Still thoughtful, he said quietly, "In a situation of this kind, Shelley, the more I know about the personalities involved, the more genuine assistance I can render. The past several hours, though they were extremely unpleasant, gave me as fine an opportunity to form opinions about and understand the people with whom we are dealing as anything I could have staged myself."

I stopped for a red light. "You could at least have told them you were supplying the bail. None of what happened would have, if you'd mentioned it."

"Please, Shelley . . . I'm trying to think. I did mention that I was posting the bond, before you arrived. Mr. Kerwin refused to accept my offer. He maintained that it was his duty and Mr. Sikkim's to furnish the bail inasmuch as Miss Wills had been an extremely loyal and conscientious employee. As soon as you came in, I knew you hadn't been successful in getting the ten thousand dollars, so it would have been rather foolish of me to mention it later."

It didn't matter now. When they'd gotten Ben up to bed and called the doctor, Kerwin had declared his intention of writing out his own personal check for the ten thousand. So that was settled. But I was curious.

"What do you mean you knew I hadn't got the money?"

"Shelley! Be quiet. How can I keep my thoughts straight if you're going to keep on interrupting me? You have a very expressive face; that was how I knew you didn't get the money!"

The light changed and I rolled ahead. I left him with his thoughts for about a half mile. Then I said, "Look, this is a very interesting murder case . . . perfumed death notes . . . a nice little counterfeit racket . . . a lovely girl in danger of having it pinned on her . . . a domineering Brahman. It's got just about everything. But there's still the little matter of a fifteen-hundred-dollar-a-week radio show that we've got to work up a script for. As much as I hate to, I'm having dinner with you, and after dinner we'll work on the script for the program."

"Didn't you tell Wakely what I told you to?"

"What?"

"That if he wouldn't advance the ten thousand dollars, I would give up the program."

I said, "Ha, ha," but it wasn't much of a laugh.

"I was serious about that, Shelley."

"You were serious? You mean you're throwing away fifteen hundred dollars a week?"

"I wouldn't care if it was fifteen thousand. I like to do business with people who have enough confidence in me to understand that if I ask for an advance of ten thousand dollars, I really need it."

I groaned. "You can't toss the show over that way, Mr. Tinney. In the first place we have a contract with Wakely. 'Either party desiring to terminate said agreement must give the other party written notice thirty days prior to the date of termination.' Remember?"

"I have broken contracts of one kind and another in every part of the world, Shelley. There are principles which cannot be written into contracts. When those principles are violated, I consider myself ethically and morally justified in breaking the contract."

"What about me?" I pleaded. "I worked hard to get this show. I stayed with you when—"

"Shelley, please. I like you, as I have often told you, a great deal. If you'll give up some of your more expensive tastes, we can do very nicely together without a radio program. You're a very capable young man. You can be a great help to me in my work. Money isn't everything."

We *might* do very nicely at that—if Mr. Tinney would only insist on a reasonable fee for his services. He had enough clients, Lord knows. But he's like the family doctor we used to have when I was a kid. If you had the money and felt like paying, it was fine. If you didn't, it was all right too.

"Money isn't everything," I said, "but it comes in mighty handy every now and then."

"I won't insist that you stay with me, Shelley. You're a smart young man. You can probably earn a great deal more money than you are earning, even at present, by handling the more orthodox type of radio talent. That girl singer you were developing, for instance."

"Nuts," I said. "You know I'll stay."

I was staying all right, but I certainly wasn't going to give up fifteen hundred dollars a week without a fight. What it needed now was babying Mr. Tinney along and getting him into the right frame of mind.

A blind man could see that Carol Wills' problem of not being in a position to marry her boy friend and the mystery of who killed Noel Landry and the problems of all parties concerned with the murder were occupying

Mr. Tinney's full attention at the moment. If I could help him straighten the whole thing put, I might be able to re-sell him a bill of goods on the Wakely program.

I decided to do everything I could to help.

Leaving the Triborough Bridge on the Manhattan side, I said, "Solved the murder yet?"

"Shelley! Don't be funny."

"I wasn't. You've hit the answers to some pretty tough ones in the years I've known you, and it didn't take you long either."

"Thank you, Shelley," he said.

He's just like a kid that way. You can lay the flattery on with a trowel and, if you do it right, he'll love it.

"Whose notes were those they found on Landry?"

"I really don't know," he said. "There is a possibility. they might have been sent to Landry himself. And then, we have already met five people directly connected with the perfume business. The notes might have been sent to any of them."

"Sikkim, Kerwin, Roche—er—ah—who are the other two?"

"Miss Wills and Frangipanni, the perfumer employed by Mr. Sikkim, the one who was arguing with him at his office when we arrived."

"Yeah, that's right."

"Then, of course, the notes would not necessarily have to be sent to someone actually engaged in the perfume business. They could have been intended for anyone with a nose."

"But Sikkim is the only one we've run into so far who admits having had business with Landry. He might have been lying about calling him in to investigate that coun-terfeit perfume racket."

"Possibly," admitted Mr. Tinney. "At any rate, Cap-tain Frieze and his associates are at the moment checking

Landry's movements in the past several days. It is likely, considering what Frieze said about Landry working every possible angle, that we'll learn of several other people who had recent dealings with him. Incidentally, did you know that Sikkim and Kerwin also own an aromatic essentials house?"

"I not only didn't know it, I don't even know what it is."

"Shelley, you are really simple about certain things. An aromatic essentials house is naturally a firm which deals in the essentials for perfumes. Oils, chemicals of one kind and another, and aromatic materials generally. The perfume business is really very fascinating."

He was leading up to something and I was beginning to suspect what it was.

"I guess so," I said.

"Did I ever tell you, Shelley, that I was in the perfume business when I was a young man, just about your age?"

"I didn't even know they used perfumes in those days."

"Shelley! Don't be disrespectful. Perfumes were in use as early as 200 B.C. Officers of the court in China, for instance, placed cloves on their tongues before talking to their ruler, so they would have a sweet breath."

"All right," I said, "tell me all about it. When you were a clerk behind the perfume counter of the village department store, what happened?"

"I wasn't a clerk, Shelley. I was a master of a gang of natives. I—"

"I knew this was coming. Natives of where?"

"Stop interrupting and I'll tell you. When I was about, oh, twenty-eight or twenty-nine, I was in Tibet, in a province called Szechuen. You've heard of musk, haven't you?"

"Yeah, it's some kind of perfume, isn't it?"

"It's a deer found in the Himalaya Mountains. The dried secretion of its preputial follicle is used in making perfumes."

"The dried secretion of what?"

". . . of the male musk deer's preputial follicle. It is one of the most powerful fixatives known to the industry." He went on and on about how he had led this gang of natives in musk deer roundups.

Finally I said, "It sounds like a hell of a way to make a living."

"Men have made sizable fortunes out of it," he said. "Do you know that approximately two ounces of the oil which is the odoriferous principle of musk sells for about fifty dollars?"

"Again I must confess my ignorance." I bowed my head in mock shame and almost ran into a taxicab.

"Look where you're going, Shelley," said Mr. Tinney.

Naturally we were late for dinner and, also naturally, Mamie raised hell. She worried about Mr. Tinney like he was her baby boy, though I'd guess he was old enough to be her father.

As I picked at the various kinds and forms of vegetables on my plate, I said, "What are you going to do about Carol Wills?"

"There isn't much we can do at the moment."

"Do you think the murder will be cleared up soon?"

"Of course, Shelley. I'm going to clear it up myself."

"You are? How?"

"In the same way that I've cleared up several thousand problems in the course of my life. I'm going to find out the underlying and true causes for the actions and reactions of the persons concerned."

"As simple as that, huh?"

"Why not? Murder is no more complex a problem than scores of others I could outline."

"Don't," I said.

Usually Mr. Tinney didn't hurry his meals. I didn't notice particularly that he was hurrying this one until Mamie said, "Mr. Tinney, stop bolting your food."

"Yes, Mamie, yes, of course," he said, and bolted some more.

From that I gathered that something was on for after dinner.

"I guess you've got a lot of correspondence to answer tonight," I said.

"Yes, Shelley, but I think I'll have to put it off until tomorrow. There's one person who might be involved in this affair whom we don't know at all."

"Who's that?"

"Frangipanni. He seemed like a terribly agitated young man this afternoon and he certainly had a disturbing effect on Mr. Sikkim. I'm curious to know why."

"You mean you're going to see him tonight?"

"Yes, and as long as you aren't eating anyway, Shelley, I wish you would look up his address in the telephone book."

"When did you last eat a piece of meat?" I asked, heading out to the living room and the phone table.

"About thirty years ago," Mr. Tinney said.

"Would this be it, do you think?" I yelled in. "Frangipanni, Enrique?"

"Probably; what's the address?"

It was over on East Twenty-fourth, one of those new apartment buildings they're putting up, I guessed.

"How many other Frangipannis are there?"

"Just two," I said, "a butcher and a florist."

"Then, of course, the first one is he."

"Why? People live in Brooklyn, the Bronx, Queens, Kings, and Richmond, too, you know." I came back into the dining room. "It would be funny," I said, "if we picked off the murderer just by going to see a guy the cops haven't even thought of yet, wouldn't it?"

"Your choice of words is bad. It would be lucky, not funny."

As it turned out, it wasn't funny. Not very.

Despite his hurrying with his meal, Mr. Tinney wanted to relax a bit after it, so he led the John Scott Trotter orchestra through a couple of numbers, using his cane for a baton. The Trotter band, as you probably know, backgrounds Bing Crosby's records, and the only music I've ever heard Mr. Tinney listen to is Bing Crosby. He has every record Crosby ever made and he's played them each— except the newer ones—at least a thousand times. He plays them to relax; he plays them when he's thinking out a particularly tough problem, and he just plays them.

It was almost ten o'clock when we started out for Frangipanni's place, and at that it was a good thing we didn't start out any later. There was no name in the slots downstairs that looked anything like Frangipanni, so I went around to the outside left of the new building and hunted up the superintendent.

"Yes, yes, he is in," that slightly shabby gentleman said. "I saw him come in about six o'clock this afternoon. And he hasn't come out since, that I know of. He has apartment 4D."

I flipped him a half dollar for thanks and went back inside and joined Mr. Tinney. We figured out which button was 4D and pressed it. Nothing happened. I finally pressed a button for a seventh-floor apartment and the door lock clicked and in we went.

"You shouldn't have done that, Shelley. Perhaps Mr. Frangipanni isn't at home and you've disturbed those other people."

"You'll never be a detective if you're going to worry about little inconveniences like that."

There was a self-service elevator and to the left of this a stairway. We got in the car and a press of the button lifted us to Four.

As we approached the door of 4D, sounds reached us as though Frangipanni were moving the furniture. They stopped suddenly and something like a groan oozed through the door as we stood directly before it.

I frowned at Mr. Tinney, who was listening intently. I pressed the buzzer: The quiet became uncomfortable. I banged on the door and still there was no answer. I could hear my own breathing, I banged again and a door opened, but not 4D. A skinny old lady stuck her head out of 4C.

"There've been some strange noises coming from there," she quavered. "I was about to call the police." And then a voice from behind 4D's door said, "Who is it?"

I didn't suppose telling the voice it was me would do much good. Mr. Tinney moved in front of me and close to the door and said, "It's Sikkim. Open the door."

"Just a second," the voice said, and the door opened.

I got a flash of a beefy face and the door started to slam shut, but Mr. Tinney's cane rammed up hard and hit the guy under the chin and I charged against the door and bowled the guy over. Lady 4C screamed and slammed her door shut.

The only light in 4D came from a lamp which had been knocked from an end table. With the oval of the shade throwing the light out in a bright, broad, cone-shaped slab, the whole thing looked like a movie set during the filming of an action sequence in a gang film.

Frangipanni, bloody and battered and very unconscious, was slumped on the floor with his head and shoulders resting against a couch on the far side of the room. The beefy boy whom Mr. Tinney had upper-cutted with his cane, and whom I'd sent sprawling, sat on his very large seat in the middle of the room and started to reach inside his coat. Another guy, small and thin, came tearing at us right through the slab of light. He had something that looked like a blackjack in his hand.

I took all this in in less than a split second, and dived for the guy on the floor. Chances were he was reaching for a gun and I figured it takes longer to beat somebody to death than shoot them.

It was a gun. He got it out just as I hit him and we rolled over and over around the floor like a couple of whirling dervishes. The punches we got in didn't do much good, but on one trip around he did lay the gun alongside my jaw and not too gently. I heard this humming sound, and even while wrestling with the guy, I thought, hell, I didn't think he hit me *that* hard.

And then the humming sound got louder and I recognized it as the same sound I'd heard so often in Mr. Tinney's room. But now Chubby was on top of me, trying to hold me still with one hand and smash the gun down on my head with the other. Over his shoulder, I saw Mr. Tinney standing where I'd left him, twirling the cane horizontally around his head so fast all you could see was a blur. The thug who'd started for him had stopped in the middle of the room like he'd frozen.

He snapped out of it as I watched, and tore at Mr. Tinney again. Mr. Tinney stopped the whirl of the cane with miraculous abruptness and, in a motion so fast I could hardly follow, brought it down with an easy snapping movement of his arm. His wrist flipped down, and though the arm and wrist motion were almost slow, there was nothing slow about the downward flick of that malacca. The tip of it touched the right wrist of the thug with the blackjack and he didn't have the blackjack any more. It dropped to the floor, and he clutched his right wrist with his left hand and screamed as though his hand had been cut off.

He bent his head to look at where it hurt, and Mr. Tinney, still holding the cane about four inches from the top in his right hand, gripped it near the point with his left and pranced in to meet the wounded thug. Like a man shoveling sand onto a high truck, he lifted the point of the cane under the small guy's chin and pitched him off to the left and behind him. The guy landed on all fours near the door, got to his feet, and ran like hell out through it.

I'd watched all this business in such complete astonishment and fascination that I'd done nothing more with my fat boy than hold him off, just by instinct. As his pal slipped through the door, Chubby managed to tear his gun arm out of my grasp and I saw the quick flash of blue-steel and tried to jerk my head out of the way. It didn't work. A bomb exploded inside my skull and the flash of blue-steel changed in rapid succession to a blazing blue-white rocket, a pinwheel of brilliant red and yellow and green, and finally to a sheet of good, clean black, and that was all.

5

Somebody was saying from far, far away, "There, he's coming around; he'll be all right, officer."

I opened my eyes and my head floated off my shoulders and up toward the ceiling of the room. I closed my eyes again and kept them that way till my head rejoined my shoulders. The voice began to sound a little closer and familiar. "Thanks very much, officer. I'm sure everything will be all right now. Mr. Shell will be up and around in a moment and we'll stay with our friend, Enrique, until we're sure he's all right."

A deeper, louder voice said, "Anything you say, Mr. Tinney. With the descriptions of those two thugs you gave us, we ought to be able to pick them up in short order."

"I'm sure you will," said Mr. Tinney's voice, and it sounded very close now. I tried opening my eyes again; my head wobbled a little and felt like it might fall off, but I kept my eyes open and the wobbly feeling left. I sat up and supported myself with my hands while the boat started to rock again. When it stopped, I looked up at Mr. Tinney and a big cop in uniform.

"Feel all right, Shelley?" Mr. Tinney asked.

"Like a million dollars, counterfeit," I said.

The big cop helped me up, held me a while, then said, "You'll be all right, son. It was a nasty smack, but there's no concussion."

The cop left. Mr. Tinney sat down in one of the deep armchairs and looked like he was going to cry.

"What's the matter with you?" I asked.

He shook his head and held his cane up to me. A little less than half his cane, I should say. It had busted about nine inches from the top.

"Oh, nuts," I said, and sat down in a chair opposite him. "What's a cane? I'll buy you another. You deserve it."

"It's not the cane, Shelley," he said sadly. "I broke it hitting that stout fellow on the head."

"You did! And what happened then?"

"He staggered toward the door and ran around to the stairs and down as fast as he could. I suppose his partner's flight robbed him of his own courage."

"Well, dammit, what're you so sorrowful about? You act like he'd shot you dead and you were mourning yourself."

"You don't understand, Shelley. As recently as six years ago, I had occasion to hit a man across the top of the head. He was the husband of a client of mine and intended to stab me. I knocked him unconscious and hardly touched him with the cane at all."

"He had a soft head," I said. "This guy didn't."

"That isn't it at all, Shelley. A properly administered flick will break a half-inch board in two with no damage to the cane whatsoever."

"Oh . . . and you should have been able to administer the flick properly and didn't?"

"Certainly, Shelley. I have always considered myself among the finest single-stickers in the world. It's a lost art. I learned it when I was little more than a boy."

A weary moan sounded from an adjoining room.

"What's that?" I asked.

"Frangipanni," whispered Mr. Tinney. "He's in the bedroom. The doctor administered a sedative. He should sleep for quite a while yet."

"Doct—"

"Shhhh . . ." cautioned Mr. Tinney.

We were silent for a few minutes.

"He's asleep," Mr. Tinney said. "The reason I didn't want you to wake him up was that I wanted to have an opportunity to look around before we talked to him."

"You said something about a doctor?"

"Of course, Shelley. You were unconscious for almost a full hour. Half the tenants in the building, the police, and a doctor were here in the meantime. The doctor tended Mr. Frangipanni, put that bandage over the gash in your temple, and left."

I felt and, sure enough, there was a bandage.

"You take the bathroom and I'll look around here in the living room," Mr. Tinney said.

The bathroom didn't look like anybody's bathroom I'd ever seen. Frangipanni hardly left himself room to move around. It was small to begin with and what there was of it was all cluttered up with jars and bottles and test tubes and mortars and pans and bunsen burners and glass and metal gadgets I'd never seen before. Some of the things had labels on them. *Phenylethyl, Alcohol, Indol, Skatol, Musk, Xylene, Orris Root,* and a lot of other fancy and semi-fancy names of oils, chemicals, powders and stuff that meant nothing to me.

These things were crowded on three tiers of a special shelf he'd built in the window. They were piled all around the wash bowl, and when I opened the medicine cabinet, that was full, too.

I looked around some more and found nothing that made sense to me, so I came out. Mr. Tinney was standing in front of a secretary. He had two pieces of paper, one in each hand. The one in his left hand he held at his side. The other he sniffed at.

"Frangipanni apparently does a lot of homework," I said. "He's got a young laboratory in the bathroom.

Mr. Tinney continued to sniff.

"Don't tell me you've found some more perfumed notes," I said as I reached for one.

He nodded. "The same perfume, too."

It was, all right. You couldn't mistake it. There was that same unpleasant odor on first quick impression, and then that peculiar combination of heavy yet soft fragrance. I read the note I'd taken from Mr. Tinney.

PERHAPS TOMORROW, PERHAPS TODAY
YOU SHALL DIE—WITH THE ODOR OF
LOVE AND HATE TO TELL YOU WHY

Beneath the message was that same strange signature, the shaky ovals and circles with long, slanted lines underneath them.

"The guy," I said, "is going in for poetry now. And not good poetry, either."

"Here's the other." Mr. Tinney handed it to me.

YOUR DEATH WILL BE SLOW AND PAIN-
FUL JUST AS WAS HERS AND MINE—BUT
IT WILL COME SOON.

And again it bore the queer hieroglyphic signature.

"This is the only one of the notes where the perfume isn't mentioned," I said. "Any reason for that?"

Mr. Tinney shrugged his shoulders.

"Did you find anything else?" I asked, returning the notes.

"I've been all through the living room, Shelley, and there isn't a thing here that looks interesting, except these notes. I went all through the desk and outside of the notes, which were in one of those pigeonholes, there isn't anything at all. I wonder if we ought to risk looking around the bedroom."

"Let's take the kitchen first," I suggested.

We did, and it was the bathroom all over again on a slightly larger scale. Bottles, and jars, test tubes and pans and vats and burners and all the other business.

"This guy," I hazarded, "must eat perfumes."

"He certainly takes a great interest in his work," said Mr. Tinney. He read the labels on some of the bottles and jars very carefully and even opened a few and sniffed them.

"Come on, expert," I said, "they don't mean any more to you than they do to me. Let's try the bedroom."

We went in softly on tiptoe. Frangipanni was sprawled out on the bed, his head swathed in bandages and a look on his face as though he was having a bad dream. He was still in his clothes and he'd kicked the covers off.

"He hasn't slept very quietly," said Mr. Tinney.

I was already at the dresser and going through the top drawer. There were shirts and handkerchiefs and other haberdashery. I got all the way down to the bottom drawer before I found anything but wearing apparel and bed sheets and pillow cases and things like that. Mr. Tinney had joined me by this time and we both saw the two small and faded photos in their joined frames. One was of a man and the other of a woman. The woman was strikingly beautiful, with deep, dark eyes that gleamed, and long, black hair set in a lustrous wave all around her face. The man was rather dark, or at least the photo made him look that way. He had eyes that held a quality of sadness, and a thick, curled-at-the-ends, handle-bar mustache. There were no markings on either side of the photos. We put them back in the drawer and started to slide it shut.

From behind us came a scream, weird and broken. I turned and flung myself at the guy on the bed and tried

to clap my hand over his mouth. I hit his eyes first, but
found his mouth in time to choke off the second scream.
He started to fight like a tiger.

"Shelley," Mr. Tinney said urgently, "leave him alone,"
and before I could, he was saying with that business in
his voice, "Mr. Frangipanni, we're your friends. We saved
you from those two men. We're here to help you. Please be
quiet. We want to talk to you."

I released my hold slowly as I felt Mr. Tinney's words
sinking in. Frangipanni had started shaking and I gripped
his shoulder, trying to steady him. We were all quiet while
he fought for control.

"Do you feel you may be able to talk now?" Mr. Tinney
asked finally,

"Who are you?" Frangipanni said, and there wasn't
much quiver in his voice.

"I'm a friend of yours. My name is Desmond Tinney
and this is Stanley Shell. A man has been murdered and—"

"Murdered?" gasped Frangipanni. "Has he been murdered?" His eyes shone. "Good! I am so glad! He should
have been murdered a long time ago!"

He spoke English very precisely, but there was a slight
accent in his speech, one that was hard to identify. Some
kind of Latin, I guessed,

Mr. Tinney said, "The police are looking for his murderer. They will probably come here to question you."

"But why? I had nothing to do with it. After I left him
I came home. I was here in my apartment all evening.
I—I—"

"He was murdered last night," I put in.

"Shelley!" exclaimed Mr. Tinney in an angry voice.

"Last night?" said Frangipanni. "Last night? But who
was it that was murdered?" He was still trembling a bit,
but seemed somehow more alert.

"Who do you think?" Mr. Tinney asked. And now I saw why he'd been angry when I told Frangipanni the murder had taken place last night.

"I—I did not think—anybody. I—was upset. I did not know what I was saying. . . ."

"That's not true, Mr. Frangipanni," said Mr. Tinney. "You thought Mr. Sikkim had been murdered . . . but we'll let it go. Noel Landry, a private detective, was killed last night."

"Landry? Landry?" muttered Frangipanni. "I am sorry, the name is not known to me."

"Are you quite sure?" asked Mr. Tinney.

"Yes, yes."

"On the gentleman's body were found two perfumed notes threatening death," said Mr. Tinney.

Frangipanni frowned at him. "I do not understand. How does that concern me?"

"Mr. Frangipanni, it would help matters if you would be more truthful. The notes found on Mr. Landry were written with the same typewriter, on the same paper, and perfumed with the same scent as these."

He took the two notes from his inside coat pocket and waved them at Frangipanni. Frangipanni grabbed for them and I slapped his arm down.

"Shelley, stop! That isn't at all necessary."

"Where did you get these notes?" asked Frangipanni. Alarm, if not fright, showed on his Latin face.

"You know where I got them, Mr. Frangipanni. In one of the pigeonholes of your desk. The question is, where did *you* get them?"

Frangipanni shrugged his shoulders, raised his hands palms up and said, "They were sent to me. They were placed beneath my door. I found them when I returned home."

"Didn't they frighten you?"

"But to be certain. They frightened me greatly. I do not know who sent them. I—I—"

"Did they come together?"

"No! First one came, then the other."

"When did the first one arrive?"

Frangipanni thought for a moment. "Saturday," he said, "two weeks ago. Then last Saturday I found the other one."

"Which came first?" Mr. Tinney asked.

Frangipanni studied them briefly. "This one," he said, and pointed to the *your death will be slow and painful* note.

"Have you notified the police?"

"No, I have not. I am a perfumer, and I feel I will be able to more readily identify the odor of the notes than the police and so possibly trace them to the sender. Then, I reason, will be time enough to notify the police."

"How do you account for the fact that similar notes were found on Mr. Landry?"

"That I cannot account for. I did not know Mr. Landry."

"So you took no steps at all to protect yourself against the sender of the notes?"

"None with the exception of my own investigation."

"Have you identified the perfume?"

"Not as yet. It is a very strange odor. It is unlike any perfume I know."

"Have you any idea who might be sending you these threats?"

"No. If I had, I should have notified the police."

"This attack on you tonight; do you think it was engineered by the person who sent you the notes?"

"It is not unlikely, but I do not know the two men who attacked me. They came in through this bedroom window, down the fire escape from the roof, I assume."

"What did they do or say when they entered?"

"One had a gun," said Frangipanni. "I was in the bathroom, working on a certain experiment, when they entered. I heard a noise, so I came out of the bathroom and met them. The one with the gun said, 'Get your hat and coat, mister, we are going places.' I refused, and the one with the gun said he would shoot me. I went to the closet in the living room for my hat and coat and they were right behind me. I reasoned that they would not risk firing the gun in the apartment because it would make a great deal of noise, so I whirled from the closet and started to fight with them. They did not shoot me but used the gun as a club and beat me with it. They—"

"Nothing more than what you've told us was said by either of the men?"

"Not one thing more."

"And you didn't recognize either of them?"

"I have never seen them before. They were strangers to me."

"May I ask, Mr. Frangipanni, how old you are?"

"Twenty-nine," said the perfumer.

"Married?"

"But no. I have always been too much occupied with my work. I have had no time for the romance and the marriage."

"One of these notes," Mr. Tinney said, waving them again, "refers to the odor of love and hate. It's supposed to tell you why you're going to die."

"It has no meaning for me," said Frangipanni quickly. "I do not understand it at all. If I did, it is possible I could say who is the sender of the notes."

"And this other one," Mr. Tinney went on, "it talks about your death being as slow and painful as 'hers' and 'mine.' You've known people who've died slowly and painfully, haven't you?"

"No, I have not. No one. The contents of the notes have no meaning for me."

"That's peculiar," said Mr. Tinney. "Usually a death threat, cryptic though it might be, makes sense at least to the person to whom it is sent."

"These have no meaning for me," repeated Frangipanni. He made a move to get out of bed. "I should like a cigarette, please. There are some in the box on the table in the living room."

"Don't disturb yourself, Mr. Frangipanni. Shelley will get them."

I went out and did and helped myself to one, the first cigarette I'd had in two months. I'd been trying to quit smoking, but this murder business was too exciting.

"My parents are both alive and well," Frangipanni was saying when I came back, "in Rome."

"This argument you were having with Mr. Sikkim this afternoon," asked Mr. Tinney, "would you mind telling me what that was about?"

I held the match for Frangipanni and he inhaled deeply before he said, "Mr. Sikkim has learned more of the experiment on which I am working, here at home. He insists that I conduct it in his laboratories and that it should become the property of the firm when I have successfully completed it. I feel it is something which I am doing in my spare time and has nothing to do with Siquin, Incorporated. If it is successful I wish to be the sole owner of it."

"Mr. Sikkim told us you were demanding a bonus."

"That is untrue."

"This experiment you're working on, can you tell us what it is?"

"I see no reason for withholding it," said Frangipanni, puffing on the cigarette nervously. "Before the war, several petroleum refiners were working with aromatic firms in an effort to develop an aromatic which will serve to overcome the unpleasant odor which distinguishes petroleum before it is refined. The petroleum industry spends a great deal of money in a very elaborate refining process which does nothing more than remove the oily odor from the fuel. The process adds nothing to the value of the fuel in any other way. Naturally, if a perfumer-chemist is able to develop an aromatic which will do the same task, it will save the petroleum industry a great deal of money and will be worth much to them."

"Do you think," asked Mr. Tinney, "that the attack on you tonight could have had anything to do with your experiments?"

Frangipanni was thoughtful for a moment. Then he said, "Mr. Sikkim is not a nice person. He would stop at nothing to get such a formula from me. But I have not yet hit upon a formula for an aromatic which would successfully perform the task. This is really my first experiment in what we term commercial perfuming. In the past I have worked almost exclusively on odors for use in powders, perfumes, creams, and similar products for personal use.

"Of recent years, however, commercial perfuming has become more and more important. Every aromatic essentials house has experts working on various phases of it. At your World's Fair, here in New York, the fishy odor of the water in Flushing Bay, which was run into the pools around the statue of George Washington and other places, was made pleasant and fragrant by an aromatic which was dropped into it. The fountain displays had always been lovely to see, but they were slightly offensive to the nose until the Fair called in a perfumer-chemist and his aromatics."

He rattled on and told us about perfumers creating the authentic underground smell in the coal mine exhibit at the Chicago Fair; about firms that used aromatics to make their advertisements more realistic and appealing; a coffee company that had its rotogravure advertisement give off the odor of freshly made coffee by mixing the proper aromatic with the printing ink.

"We get the idea, Mr. Frangipanni," Mr. Tinney said finally, "but you don't believe these notes or the attack on you had anything to do with your experiments?"

"I cannot say for certain. I am inclined to think not."

"You've been very nice, Mr. Frangipanni," said Mr. Tinney, "and for that reason I don't like to have to tell you this. But it will be necessary for me to turn these notes over to Captain of Detectives Henry Frieze, who is investigating Mr. Landry's murder. Since similar notes were found—"

"To be certain," said Frangipanni. "That will be all right. Since the attack on me tonight, I should welcome protection by the police department."

"You'll get it," said Mr. Tinney, "but there's one other thing I must tell you. Captain Frieze's detectives have been checking on the movements of Noel Landry just before his death. Captain Frieze said that among the persons visited by Mr. Landry was one Enrique Frangipanni."

"But it is not true. I did not know Landry!"

"I wouldn't advise you to try to tell Captain Frieze that," said Mr. Tinney. "He knows better. And if you refuse to admit the truth he might suspect the reason to be that you killed Mr. Landry yourself."

"It is ridiculous," said Frangipanni. The alarm on his face was pronounced. "Landry came here yesterday for the first time. I had seen him at our laboratories during his visits to Mr. Sikkim. I learned he was a private detective and I asked him to see me here yesterday. I wanted his help in tracing the sender of these notes, so—"

"How did you find out he was a private detective?" asked Mr. Tinney.

"I met him in a restaurant near the offices one day and we had a conversation. He told me so himself."

"I see," said Mr. Tinney. "So the notes found on his person had originally been sent to you?"

"Yes, and I turned them over to him to aid him in his investigation."

"You turned them over to him yesterday?"

Frangipanni nodded. "Yesterday afternoon."

"How long ago did you receive the two notes you turned over to him?"

Frangipanni thought for several minutes again, then said, "They came, one after another, on Saturdays. The first came a month ago, the second a week later."

"And you waited a full month before you decided to call someone in to help you?"

"Yes. I thought at first I could trace the notes myself. When a month passed, and I made no progress, I reasoned it would be better if I called in a man whose business it was to trace such things."

"Why didn't you call in the regular police?"

"Because I did not want the person who was sending the notes to suspect that I had called in the police."

"That's very weak," said Mr. Tinney, "but it's all right with me. How it will be with Captain Frieze I couldn't say. The few facts you have told us, however, open up another interesting possibility."

"What is that?" asked Frangipanni.

"That Mr. Landry might have discovered who was sending you those threatening notes and that that person might have murdered Mr. Landry in order to prevent him from passing the information on to you."

"Perhaps, but—"

"In which case, Mr. Frangipanni, you yourself might still be murdered at any moment."

6

"Interesting young man, that Frangipanni," said Mr. Tinney as the car rolled homeward.

"A hell of a liar," I commented. "How did you know Landry'd been up to see him?"

"From the notes, of course. They're so similar, there was a good chance a person possessing one would know any person possessing others."

"Then Frieze didn't tell you that Landry had called on Frangipanni at all?"

"Of course not. You were with me practically all the time I was with Frieze. Incidentally, as soon as we get to my home, we'll have to call him and tell him we have these notes and about our talk with Frangipanni."

"I thought," I said, "you were going to solve this murder yourself."

"I am, but I certainly am not going to do anything to interfere with Captain Frieze's investigation."

"I wish you'd turn the whole thing over to him and get together with me tomorrow to work up a script for next week's show. Wakely insists on seeing one."

"Shelley! I told you there would be no more show. Now please be quiet, while I try to work out the significance of the various points we discussed with Mr. Frangipanni."

I saw he wasn't sweetened up enough yet to listen to anything more about the program.

"Tell me about the cane and the single-sticking first," I said. I was really interested and I hoped to do a little more selling on him by letting him brag a bit.

"Oh, that," he said deprecatingly. "As I started to tell you at Mr. Frangipanni's place, it's a lost art. From the sixteenth to the eighteenth centuries it had quite a vogue in England. They taught it to the youngsters in school, as a matter of fact. It served as fine elementary training in fencing, although I have always been of the opinion that a cane can be even more effective than a sword."

"You're not that old, are you?"

"How do you mean, Shelley?"

"I mean you weren't a youngster during the sixteenth or eighteenth century when they were teaching this single-sticking . . ."

"Don't be absurd, Shelley. Of course not. Strangely enough, I learned it from an Apache in Paris many years ago. I lived in the Montmartre section of Paris for quite a while. Pierre, this Apache, and I became very close friends. He never carried any weapons except a little parasol. And he was feared by every Apache in the district. I saw him engage in fights with other Apaches armed with knives and even occasionally a gun, and he never came off second best."

"He must have been quite a single-sticker."

"He was indeed. When he started that little parasol in a *moulinet,* the boys who knew him ran for cover."

"A mouliwhat?"

"A *moulinet.* That's the term for the action of twirling the cane horizontally overhead. It's the basic movement in single-sticking, the position from which all flicks, jabs, flips and cuts are administered. I once saw Pierre fight four opponents. Two of them he disposed of by opening their scalps. He broke the third one's wrist and pitched the fourth clear over his head and out the door of the cafe."

"Just like you did with that little thug tonight."

"Just as I *attempted* to do," corrected Mr. Tinney sadly. "Age does take its toll."

"You did all right," I said. "You got rid of those two thugs."

"That's the trouble. If I had captured them we might have learned a great deal more about the murder of Noel Landry. Now please, Shelley, let me think this situation out."

He didn't have much time for it, because in another fifteen minutes we pulled up in front of the house.

"I don't think I'll come in," I said. "I'm starved and I'm tired. I want to get home."

"Please, Shelley. I want you to take care of calling Captain Frieze for me. You can leave right after you make the call."

"All right," I agreed, although I didn't like it.

When we got into the living room I learned the real reason he wanted me to come in. Mamie came down from her bedroom looking like the wrath of God, and glared at Mr. Tinney and me.

"It's close to one o'clock, Mr. Tinney," she said. "Are you trying to kill yourself? You should have been in bed three hours ago." Mamie is the only person I've ever met who can bulldoze Mr. Tinney.

"Well, you see, Mamie . . ." he started to say.

"And as for you, Shelley, you should know better than to keep Mr. Tinney out till this hour. Sure, and you haven't the sense you were born with."

"Look, Mamie," I said, "Mr. Tinney is free, white, and a hundred and one. If he thinks he wants to stay out till one o'clock he ought to—"

"Never mind your fresh remarks, Shelley. Please, Mr. Tinney, go to bed."

"Right away, Mamie. I have a few things I have to discuss with Shelley first."

I could see why Mr. Tinney had never married. A wife *and* a housekeeper like Mamie Hannigan would have been too much. Mamie grunted and pounded her way back upstairs, loud enough to let us know she was madder than hell with both of us.

I walked to the phone and called police headquarters and asked for the Homicide Bureau and Captain Frieze. I was amazed to find he was still there. I told him Mr. Tinney wanted to talk to him and he said he'd be over as soon as he finished checking some reports.

Mr. Tinney had put Crosby's *Lilacs in the Rain* on the phonograph and had it turned down very low and was sitting in his favorite chair, looking thoughtful.

"Shelley, would you get me a glassful of my juice? Mamie would have gotten it for me if she hadn't been so angry."

I went and got it.

"The trouble with this case, Shelley," he said when I came back, "is that there are too many motives. That photo of Carol and Jimmy Knight; the perfumed death threat notes, talking about love and indicating certainly an affair between a man and a woman; the counterfeit bottle and label racket; the aromatic experiment on which Frangipanni is working. Any one or more of them may have some bearing on the murder of Noel Landry. You'll recall that Frieze told us he was commonly known as 'Angles.'"

"I recall," I said, and watched him drink-munch that evil-looking vegetable concoction.

"A man like Landry, thrown into a situation of this kind, would be moving around so fast and working so many angles it would be next to impossible to trace them with any degree of accuracy." He paused for another sip. "I'm more than ever convinced," he continued, "that the only thing to do is the thing I've been doing for years and years with the thousands of problems which have been brought to me. I'm just going to have to learn as much as possible about each of the personalities we have encountered and determine the murderer on the basis of those personalities."

"You mean you have no idea who the murderer is yet?"

"I have some ideas but they could just as easily be wrong as right. We still don't know enough about the people concerned."

"If you're going to stand around waiting to get to know every one of them intimately," I said, "the murderer is liable to die of old age."

"Such remarks are entirely unnecessary, Shelley. I don't mean I'm going to try to learn to know them all intimately. I mean people's lives begin the day they are born. Their actions and reactions, under a given set of circumstances in later years, are largely determined by the conditioning of their earlier years. One can get a much truer picture of a person's character by looking back into that person's past than by living with him every day for years during his later life."

"I guess you're right," I said, "but I'm hungry."

The needle started to scratch on the uncut wax of the *Lilacs* thing. I went over and lifted it.

"Want the other side?" I asked.

"Of course," said Mr. Tinney.

In a minute Crosby was giving out with *Trade Winds*.

"Do we work on the program tomorrow?" I asked.

"We do not, Shelley; please don't keep asking me about that."

We argued about it, then kicked the murder around, then argued some more. I got nowhere. Mamie came down and growled at us and made nasty cracks at me a half dozen times, trying to get Mr. Tinney to go to bed. But it was no good. Radio show or no radio show, murder or no murder, I started to yawn. But not Mr. Tinney. Frieze had evidently gotten tied up at headquarters, because it was almost three o'clock before the door chimes bonged and I let him in.

"Hello, Hank," said Mr. Tinney. "Sit down."

Frieze did, like a very weary man. He took out a pack of cigarettes.

I said, "Can I have one, Captain?"

"Sure. Sorry." He tossed one over to me, lit his and tossed me the matches.

"What have you got, Mr. Tinney?"

"Some more notes," Mr. Tinney said, and took them out of his pocket.

Frieze got up and walked across to Mr. Tinney and took the notes. He sniffed them and studied them carefully. "They're the same all right. What corpse did you find these on?"

"No corpse," said Mr. Tinney, and told Frieze the whole story of what had happened at Frangipanni's—all except how he'd routed the two thugs with the cane. He made me the hero of that episode with, I was sure, an ulterior motive. He also gave Frieze a complete and very accurate description of Frangipanni.

By this time Crosby had finished *Blues in the Night* and I shut off the phonograph altogether. It was very quiet, while Frieze digested what Mr. Tinney had given him.

"That's one guy we missed," he said, referring to Frangipanni. "Could I use your phone, Mr. Tinney? I want to get a couple of the boys to go right over and pick up this Frangipanni."

Mr. Tinney nodded and Frieze made his call.

"Have you been able to find Jimmy Knight yet?" Mr. Tinney asked then.

Frieze shook his head. "Not yet, but we were pretty lucky in checking on Landry. One of the stoolies, a guy we've only had working for us a little while, talked to Landry about a week ago. Like I told you, Landry was asking around about some of the old alky boys. Landry's been seeing everybody in this setup. He was out at Roche's house day before yesterday. He saw old man Sikkim three, four times—at the office and out at his Great Neck place. Now, with this Frangipanni, that leaves only Mrs. Sikkim, her son, and Kerwin that Landry didn't have dealings with. And as far as that goes, he might have seen Mrs. Sikkim and the boy out at Great Neck and he might have seen Kerwin on any one of his calls to the office. This is the damnedest case!"

"What did Landry see Roche about?"

"The same thing he saw Sikkim about," said Frieze. "He wanted the association to pay him to find the perfume packaging counterfeiters. Roche says he turned him down cold. The association couldn't afford to hire private operatives. Roche, as executive secretary, works on it himself as best he can and for the rest they leave it up to the city cops."

"Why didn't Roche mention his connection with Landry at Sikkim's this afternoon?"

"The obvious reason. He didn't want to get mixed up in it, if it was at all possible. Trouble with this case is, the people are too substantial. You can't push them around any. And when you can't push, it's hell getting people to open up."

"We'll have to do the best we can without pushing," said Mr. Tinney. "I never believed in it, anyway."

"You never tried to find a murderer," Frieze said.

Mr. Tinney changed the subject abruptly. "Did you find out whether Landry actually made a contact with any of the boys from the old bootlegging days, the ones he was asking about?" he said.

"We've dragged in all six of them. They're all in different rackets now. Manny Feldman, of our Main Office

Squad, knows what they do practically every minute of the
day and night and he vouched for what they told us. There
isn't a one of 'em has anything to do with a counterfeit
perfume racket. I don't know whether Sikkim was telling
the truth, about that or not."

"It's hard to say, Hank," said Mr. Tinney. "How about
the perfume manufacturers' list he had? Has anything been
done on that?"

"Sure; the whole squad's been working on this thing.
Landry saw three of the perfume manufacturers on the
list. I guess that's all he was able to get around to before
he got knocked over. Or else some of the others are lying.
The three he talked to all say the same thing. He asked
them two questions: whether they'd be interested in paying to find out who was running the counterfeit perfume
racket, and what they'd be willing to pay for a formula
for an aromatic that'd take the stink out of unrefined oil.
That's the one your Frangipanni was working on."

"Mr. Landry certainly didn't pass up anything, did he?"

"Hell, no."

"Did any of the perfume manufacturers hire him?"

"They all say no, but now that the guy's been knocked
off they'd say that, anyway."

"How about this O'Hara you were going to look up,"
asked Mr. Tinney, "the name Landry had in that note-
book?"

"We've looked him up," said Frieze. "He's got himself
some kind of cockeyed deal with the Cuban government.
He's been in Havana the last four months. I guess we can
eliminate him."

"Is Cuba a center for any kind of perfume oil or something?" I asked.

"Shelley!" said Mr. Tinney. "Don't be smart. It's hard
enough to eliminate anyone from this case without having
you try to keep in it persons who can safely be eliminated."

"This perfume business," I said, "looks so screwy to me, you never know where anything might pop up. You told me about that musk business yourself. I'm just trying to cover all the possibilities."

Frieze chuckled without much mirth. "It'd take a pretty big tent to cover 'em all. There's one more that I haven't even mentioned yet—this stoolie I was telling you about. On Wednesday he followed Landry to an apartment house down in Greenwich Village on Jane Street. He saw Landry talking to the super of this house and slipping him some dough. We checked the names of every tenant in the house and we had the super downtown. None of the tenants' names mean anything as far as I can see. With the super we had a chance to push a little, but it didn't help. He's a tight-lipped bastard, who just won't crack. He claims Landry asked him for the same thing we did, a list of the tenants, and gave him five bucks for it. That's all."

"Why wouldn't Landry just look in the slots under the bells?" I asked. "That would give him the same information, wouldn't it?"

"Not quite," said Mr. Tinney. "Don't you remember at Frangipanni's house? He didn't have his name in the slot."

"That's right," I said.

"I've got men questioning the tenants, floor by floor," Frieze said, "but it's going to take time."

"Please, may I have the address, Hank?" Mr. Tinney asked.

"Sure." He gave it to us and I wrote it down. "But listen, Mr. Tinney, I'd be careful if I were you. There's at least one person running around loose who's already carved a piece out of a guy and who won't hesitate carving some more if anybody gets too close. You're liable to get hurt."

"Oh, Shelley will take care of me," Mr. Tinney said, grinning at me.

"Sure," I said, "as long as Mr. Tinney has a cane, I'll take care of him."

"What do you mean?" Frieze asked.

I told him what had really made those two thugs run.

"Keerist!" he exclaimed when I'd finished. "What are you doing, Mr. Tinney, holding out on me?"

We sat around and talked some more and then the phone rang. I walked over and lifted it out of its cradle.

"Hello," I said.

A rich feminine voice, straining for control, said, "Mr. Tinney? Is Mr. Tinney there?"

"Just a minute," I said. "Who is this?"

"Mrs. Amerandra Sikkim," the voice answered. "Please, is Mr. Tinney there?"

"Yes, just a minute," I said, and held the phone out to Mr. Tinney. "It's Mrs. Sikkim, and she sounds excited."

He came over and took the phone. "Hello, Mrs. Sikkim," he said quietly. Then, "I see. . . Yes. . . certainly. . . . Yes . . . I'll come right out." He replaced the phone in its cradle. There was a very worried expression in his keen blue eyes.

"What's up?" asked Frieze.

"Something terrible has happened out at the Sikkim place," Mr. Tinney said quietly. "Something Mrs. Sikkim would rather not discuss over the telephone. She asked me to come out right away."

We went out and climbed into my car.

"What the hell could have happened now?" Frieze asked.

"I'll bet it's that batty Ben again," I hazarded.

"Why would she call you, Mr. Tinney?" Frieze said, puzzled. "You just met her tonight. You didn't talk to her more than fifteen minutes altogether while I was there."

"Listen, Captain," I said, "I've seen people talk to Mr. Tinney five minutes and turn the family jewels over to him for safekeeping."

"I know, I know," Frieze said, "but it's after three o'clock. Ladies like Mrs. Sikkim don't call casual acquaintances at this hour unless something pretty bad's happened."

"Yes, you're right, Hank," said Mr. Tinney. "I'm afraid Amerandra Sikkim has been murdered."

7

"What makes you say that?" asked Frieze, after the echo of the bombshell had cleared.

"I may be wrong," said Mr. Tinney, "but . . ."

"Yeah, I may be an Afghanistan," I muttered under my breath. He's been wrong on minor guesses, but on damned few of them. On major prognostications, never.

"What did you say, Shelley?" he asked.

"Nothing, nothing at all."

"Well, stop grumbling. You see, Hank, to begin with, if anything happened to the house or any part of the house, like a fire or something of that sort, Mrs. Sikkim would hardly consider it terrible enough to call me in the middle of the night. So the something that happened must have happened to a person. There are just two persons who would be at the house at this hour about whom Mrs. Sikkim would be enough concerned to take the action she did—her husband and her son.

"If it were her son, whom she loves very dearly, she wouldn't have been able to muster the self-control she did on the telephone. Her voice had nothing of sorrow in it, as a matter of fact. Just a tenseness, a kind of excitement. So let's assume it's her husband. Her love for her husband died long ago. I could see that by watching both of them at the questioning this afternoon. If something 'terrible,' as she described it, happened to him, it would have to be something really terrible to make her phone me in the middle of the night. I can't think of anything which would fit the true sense of the word 'terrible,' as used by a woman with Mrs. Sikkim's reserve, as well as murder. But I could be wrong."

"That's pretty fancy figuring," said Frieze. "I didn't notice there was anything particularly wrong between Mr. and Mrs. Sikkim this afternoon."

"You couldn't very well have noticed. After all, it was you who was doing the questioning. You couldn't have been talking to one person and watching another. But all during your interrogations, and especially during the rather violent argument between Sikkim and Randolph Kerwin, I saw very clearly that Mrs. Sikkim's sympathy lay with Kerwin. And when Sikkim and the boy were having it out, Mrs. Sikkim's eyes absolutely blazed hatred at her husband. The trouble with you, Hank, is that you were watching Sikkim and his son. During the course of the several arguments I had ample opportunity to watch every person in the room at one time or another."

"I can see how I might have missed some of it," Frieze admitted, "but I still say it's fancy figuring."

"I have one other reason for making what seems to be such a wild guess. The really important reason. Amerandra Sikkim is quite a ruthless man. I have observed at least four people since this morning who I imagine hated him enough to kill him."

"You're certainly a hell of an observant gent, Mr. Tinney!"

"I've been solving people's problems almost exclusively on the basis of my observations of their actions for some fifty-four years," said Mr. Tinney.

Frieze said, "I hope your guess is wrong this time."

"If it is . . . murder," mused Mr. Tinney, "I hope Carol wasn't near the Sikkim place when it happened."

"I doubt that she was," said Frieze. "She's still in jail. Ryan rushed that charge through and showed the judge enough for him to decide to hold her without bond."

Mr. Tinney looked surprised and hurt. "You could have called me, Hank."

Frieze said, "I've been so busy all day I haven't even been able to think. Besides, it's better that the girl's in jail. Keeps her out of mischief."

The minute we hit the long road up to the Sikkim place we could see *something* was wrong. The house was lit up like a ball park with a night game. As we pulled around behind the four or five other cars in front, two figures came running toward us, one tall and broad, the other small and slim. They turned out to be Mrs. Sikkim and Randolph Kerwin. Both wore topcoats; Mrs. Sikkim's over a nightgown, and Kerwin's over his regular clothes.

They merely nodded to Captain Frieze and me, but Mrs. Sikkim said to Mr. Tinney, "It's Mr. Sikkim. He's—he's dead."

There was no grief in her voice nor on her aristocratically featured face—just an anxiety that showed in her eyes and the drawn mouth.

"He was murdered," Kerwin cut in. "Someone stabbed him and—and threw the body in the pool."

That's where the crowd was. We walked over and watched a small, sour-faced man bending over something under a blanket at the edge of the pool. It must have been Sikkim's body. The butler I'd met that afternoon was there with a coat over his pajamas. There were also two policemen in uniform and two in plainclothes. I can't say how I knew these last two were policemen, except that they looked different from the four men who surrounded them and who turned out to be reporters.

One of the detectives, a guy about six feet four, who looked like he'd still be six feet four if he laid on his side,

pushed out of the group and came to meet us. He was
so big that the four reporters who started to follow him
looked like poodles yapping at the heels of a Great Dane.

"What're you doing, Mrs. Sikkim, inviting all your
friends to this shindig?" he barked sarcastically. Mrs.
Sikkim flinched but said nothing. Then the big dick saw
Frieze. "You're in the wrong county, Frieze," he said. "This
is my party." His voice was as big as his body and he didn't
do anything to tone it down.

"Take it easy, Taggert. This might tie in with the Landry
kill. No reason we can't work together."

One of the reporters stepped out. "Are you Captain
Frieze of Manhattan homicide? How's the Landry investigation coming?"

The other three took it up and the questions spurted
out of them like water out of four leaks in the same hose.

"What's the tie-in, Captain?"

"Did Sikkim know Landry?"

"Who killed Landry?"

Frieze held up his hand. "Sorry, boys. Nothing's happened yet. I don't even expect an arrest within twenty-four
hours."

"Maybe *you* don't," barked Taggert, "but I'm working
this end. There'll be an arrest within twenty-four hours."

Frieze spoke softly. "Maybe there will at that. You
ought to know all about it; you've spent about an hour on
the case already."

Taggert moved forward, hunched over like a wrestler
walking in for the kill. Frieze stood there and looked up
into his eyes.

"Listen, Frieze," the big cop said when Frieze refused
to give ground, "if you want to work with me on this,
don't be a smart boy."

Frieze said, "We'll work together. I don't know how,
but we will. We'll have to."

He walked past Taggert and you couldn't get a hair between them. He continued on toward the little man who was just rising from the corpse.

"Wait a minute, Frieze," Taggert yelled after him, as Mr. Tinney and I started to follow the group across the lawn toward the body. "Who are these two?"

"Mr. Tinney and Mr. Shell have already helped my case. I think they can help me even more. If you don't mind, I'd like them to sit in."

Taggert figured Frieze might start to ask the medical examiner some questions before he could, so he just grunted at us and hurried forward. Frieze never intended to do any questioning. Not for the moment, anyway. He simply leaned over, lifted the sheet from the corpse and took a fleeting look.

Taggert said, "What's the dope, Doc?"

The sour-faced medical examiner answered crisply, "Knife wound. Just one. Pierced the heart. Must have died instantly. Near as I can judge, it happened between twelve and two a.m. Body in water more than an hour, I'd say."

He marched off as another car roared into the driveway. Two men with a wicker basket came along and took the blanket and the thing under it away.

"Well, let's get inside and get started," Taggert said.

In the big library, where the meeting had been held the previous afternoon, Frieze said, "I'd like to make a suggestion, Taggert. We've been working on this job steady since early yesterday morning. We've picked up a little stuff. I'll go over it with you and—"

"Yeah, that'll be all right, I guess," Taggert said. "Bush," he called to one of the cops, "take everybody out into that other room, I'll call them in one at a time when I need 'em."

We followed the officer—all of us except the reporters and the other detective, who was apparently Taggert's stooge. They just sat.

"Sorry, boys," said Frieze, to the newsmen, "but the investigation isn't far enough along yet to release anything. Y'mind?"

The reporters moved toward the door, but Taggert barked, "I want the boys to stay. They've got jobs . . ."

Frieze said, "Okay, boys, you can stay." He came toward the door himself.

"Where you going?" yelled Taggert. "You can't withhold information that might—"

"I won't withhold it," Frieze said coldly, "but I won't have every move we've made and are planning to make spread all over the newspapers. Some murderers can read, you know."

Taggert made an angry noise in his throat," but said, "All right, boys. I'll see you later."

The reporters came to the door and, just before it closed, I heard Frieze say in that flat, cold voice of his, "Listen, Taggert, if you screw up this investigation by spilling anything I tell you to those reporters, I'll take care of you myself."

What Taggert answered only sounded like a series of loud growls through the heavy oak door. I wished I could have stayed for the fun.

The butler stood in a corner of the room. The cops fidgeted around, looking professional, and Kerwin, Mrs. Sikkim and Mr. Tinney walked over to a sofa that was covered with some kind of blue and white striped material that looked like silk. The reporters, who'd come out of the library after me, were on top of them before they even sat down. They started to pop questions at Mrs. Sikkim. Her eyes pleaded with them to let up.

Kerwin voiced his plea. "Gentlemen, please. If you'll give Mrs. Sikkim a chance to recover from the shock of this thing, she'll be glad to talk to you."

Without seeming to, they ignored Kerwin and went right on popping questions.

Mr. Tinney said, "Boys, I'd like to make a suggestion if I might. You'll be able to do much more comprehensive and intelligent stories, not only on this case but on the Landry murder, if you'll take advantage of this opportunity to get the real inside dope on it. None of it has been released to the New York papers yet and—"

"What do you mean?" they said, like a quartette in a minstrel show.

He gestured with his head, indicating that they were to come closer. They crowded around him and he whispered something to them. I couldn't hear what he said, but it wasn't long before I got a pretty good idea. He stopped whispering and the newspapermen came for me in a rush.

"Come on, Mr. Shell, open up." "Give us this perfume background." "Be a regular guy. We won't print anything you ask us to keep confidential."

A glance over their shoulders told me Mr. Tinney was already in earnest conversation with Mrs. Sikkim and Kerwin. All three of them were talking, low-toned but animatedly. I'll do this, I thought, but Foxy Grandpa better do that radio show Tuesday night.

The telephone rang and the butler moved quietly across the room to answer it.

"Yes . . ." he said. "One moment, please." He turned toward the blue and white striped sofa. "It's for you, Mr. Tinney."

Mr. Tinney's words barely reached me as he spoke softly into the telephone. "Hello . . . yes . . . yes, Mamie, No, I didn't get any message. No. . . . He is? Fine. Have him wait. Don't permit him to leave under any circumstances . . . Yes . . . Good-bye, Mamie." He replaced the phone and walked back to the couch.

The reporters leaped toward him again and started to ask questions about the call.

"Please, boys," he said. "It's nothing at all. Just a client of mine to see me. Please . . ."

They persisted for a time, but when Mr. Tinney isn't giving out, he just isn't giving out. He brushed them off and walked over to the butler and had a brief whispered conversation with him. Then he returned to his conference on the couch. The reporters came over to me again.

"All right, fellows," I said, and led them from where I'd been sitting to a nice, soft-looking armchair on the other side of the room from where Mr. Tinney was working. I made myself very comfortable. They had paper and pencil out and they practically sat in my lap as I talked.

"These notes," I said, "with the strange perfume. They were found on Landry's body—"

"We know that," one of them said. "What about them?"

"I'm telling you. Be a little patient. We have a pretty good idea just what the perfume is. You see, in Tibet there's a small province called Szechuen. This province is where musk comes from. You boys know what musk is, don't you?"

I went on and on like that. I led them through a musk hunt that covered practically every cranny and crevice of the Himalayas. I gave them lurid descriptions of what happened to poor Mr. Musk after we rounded him up. I even added a few incidentals that seemed like a good idea at the moment, but what would probably be news to a real musk hunter. All of which took considerable time—enough time, anyway, to give not only Mr. Tinney a chance to talk to Mrs. Sikkim and Kerwin, but to let Frieze finish the scenario for his friend, Taggert, Or I guess he did, anyway, because before I had finished, Taggert swung back one side of the big oak door and said, "Mrs. Sikkim, I'd like to talk to you now."

She got up and I'll be a male musk deer myself if she didn't seem a lot less tense than before Mr. Tinney had talked to her. She walked with that straight-backed, chin-up way of hers into the library. Mr. Tinney continued to talk with Kerwin.

I must have been good, because the reporters wanted more, which I gladly gave them. From the musk saga, I went on to tell them about the plans that'd been found on Landry for a secret formula for perfuming poison gas. Toward the end of this story I think the boys were beginning to get on to the fact that they were being ribbed. They were looking at me with what might have been called open suspicion. But by then it was too late. Kerwin had had his turn with the detectives and so had the butler.

The three of them came out with the butler, and Taggert walked over to the sofa where Mrs. Sikkim, Kerwin and Mr. Tinney were sitting.

"I want to talk to your son, Mrs. Sikkim," he said. "D'you want to have him come down or shall I go up?"

Mrs. Sikkim got up quickly, panic in her eyes. "You can't. I'm sorry, but I can't permit it. My son is not at all well. We had the doctor for him this afternoon."

"I don't think it would hurt him to talk a little," argued Taggert.

"I absolutely won't permit it, Captain Taggert. You have no right—"

"What's your doctor's name and phone number?" Taggert asked relentlessly.

"See here, Captain," Kerwin put in, "can't this wait until morning? The boy is on the verge of a nervous collapse. A shock like this might—well, it might have serious consequences."

"What's the number, Mrs. Sikkim?" Taggert said again.

Frieze said, "Mrs. Sikkim, if the captain wasn't dead right I'd stop this myself. But there's been a murder, the second murder in two days. We can't take any chances. If your doctor says it'll hurt the boy if we talk to him, we won't, but we'll have to know from the doctor."

Mrs. Sikkim told the doctor's name and number in a dull, dead voice. Taggert picked up the phone, gave the number, and glared while he waited for the doctor.

"Hello, Doctor Robinson? This is Captain Dave Taggert of the Nassau County Homicide Bureau. Mr. Amerandra Sikkim's just been murdered. That's right, murdered. It's important that we talk to his son about it as soon as possible. Can we wake him now?"

He listened, the scowl on his face deepening. "Yeah, but look, Doctor," he said finally, "this is murder. Somebody killed Sikkim, We can't horse around on these things. . . . What? Yeah, sure . . . naturally, we'll take it easy. . . . Yeah, yeah . . . okay."

A grin that wasn't nice was on his face as he replaced the phone. "The boy's all right," he said. "All we got to do is take it a little easy."

"If you like, Mrs. Sikkim," Frieze said, "you can go up and wake him yourself. You can—can kind of tell him about it."

"Wait a minute," Taggert objected. "What is this, Frieze? I'm breaking it to him. I want to see how he reacts. It might be important."

Frieze walked to the stairs, put a foot on the first step and cupped his left hand over the bronze ball of the bottom balustrade. He jerked his head toward the winding staircase and said, "Go on up, Mrs. Sikkim, if you want to."

Mrs. Sikkim flashed him a look of gratitude and walked toward the stairs. Taggert walked after her, looking as though he was going to grab her from behind any second. She made it to the stairs and started up. Taggert stopped at the foot of the stairs and watched her ascend. He glowered at Frieze, speechless with anger.

"You can't get away with this, Frieze," he bellowed. "You're obstructing justice. You're—"

"Obstructing hell!" Frieze said in a low, flat whisper. "If the kid killed him, his mother talking to him first won't stop us from finding out."

"This is my case, Frieze. You can't come down here and start running the show your way."

"I'm not trying to run anything, Taggert. It's your case, but be a little human."

Taggert made that angry noise in his throat again, whirled and stalked, away from Frieze, saying dirty words under his breath. Frieze looked after him, shaking his head sadly. Nobody said anything and nobody did anything, except a few of us fidgeted, waiting for Mrs. Sikkim to show up again. We waited two minutes, three, four. . . .

Frieze took out a cigarette and the scrape of the match as he lit it was like a shot.

Taggert, who was stalking up and down the floor like a tiger in a cage, stopped and glared at Frieze.

"I'm going up, Frieze," he said, and started for the stairs. And he meant it. You could tell by the long-legged, hard-heeled way he strode across the room.

Frieze stepped away from the balustrade and stood directly in the center of the first step, with his legs spread wide apart and his arms hanging loosely at his sides. Taggert reached him and looked up over his head toward the top of the stairs. We all looked up. Frieze turned his head and looked.

Mrs. Sikkim stood there with her left hand holding the railing. She swayed and Frieze ran up to her, taking the steps three at a time.

"I'm all right," she murmured in an unsteady voice. "I'm all right. . . . My son is not in his room. I—I—I looked in the other rooms. He's not in—any of them."

Taggert said, "I knew it, dammit, I knew it!"

Randolph Kerwin started past him up the stairs and met Mrs. Sikkim and Frieze coming down. Taggert's stooge, the cops, the reporters and I gaped.

Mr. Tinney went to the phone table, got out the directory and started to leaf through it. He found what he wanted, picked up the phone and gave the number to the operator.

Taggert led the way toward him, shouting, "Now, what the hell are you doing?"

Mrs. Sikkim, supported by Kerwin and Frieze, walked over to the blue and white striped couch.

"Hello," Mr. Tinney said presently. "Is this the Women's House of Detention? I'm calling for Captain Henry Frieze. Is— What? . . . Yes, just a moment."

He lowered the phone to his side and said quietly to Frieze, "There's been a jail break, Hank. They've been trying to reach you for the past hour."

8

You've got to hand it to Frieze. He didn't scream "What!" or anything silly like that. He simply moved to Mr. Tinney's side fast, took the telephone, did a lot more listening than talking, and finally hung up. There was a bitter, disillusioned look on his usually inexpressive face as he turned back to us.

Taggert, who'd been stalking up and down with fierce futility, bellowed, "Will someone tell me what the hell is going on around here?"

Frieze said with quiet bitterness in his voice, "Ben Sikkim wheedled his way into the Women's House of Detention and busted out of there with Carol Wills about an hour ago."

"Isn't that the dame you've been holding for the Landry murder?" growled Taggert.

Frieze nodded and picked up the telephone again. He called Centre Street and in a flat voice told somebody to change the pick-up order on Ben Sikkim and Carol Wills, which had already gone out, to "wanted for double murder: Noel Landry in Manhattan on October 13th and Amerandra Sikkim in Nassau on the 15th."

Then he walked over to a chair where he had thrown down his hat, picked it up and started to walk out. As we followed, Taggert started to say, "I'll have men around this house day and night, so if any of you want to leave . . ."

Outside in the car Frieze said, "I never should have been a cop. I feel too damn sorry for people. Everything in the world pointed to that Wills kid's guilt, and I go soft on her. I play along with Mrs. Sikkim and try to give her and her son an even break . . . and what happens? That young madman has to crash the girl out of the clink and— by the way, Mr. Tinney, what made you call the clink?"

"The last time we saw Ben he had just one idea in his mind—to get Carol out of jail. I thought he might have gone there when he wasn't home," explained Mr. Tinney. Then he added, "You haven't changed your mind about Miss Wills' innocence of the murder, have you, Hank?"

"No, but I've pretty definitely made it up about her boy friend. I think he killed Landry yesterday and knocked off his old man today. They've been scrapping about that girl so long the boy's practically lost his mind."

"There's no point in jumping at conclusions, Hank," said Mr. Tinney. "I think if Ben killed his father he would have come right to the police and confessed. That's the frame of mind he's in."

"He is, eh! I didn't tell you that he wielded a jackknife when he crashed out with the girl. It was the knife and the wild look of the guy that got him through."

I groaned, "Oh . . . ohhh."

Mr. Tinney said, "If you will come to my home with us right now, Hank, we should be able to learn a little more about the entire case. Jimmy Knight has been waiting for me for more than an hour."

"He has?"

"Yes. Mamie heard us talking about Mrs. Sikkim just before we left and figured we had gone out there. She'd called several times before we got there and left word for me to call her back as soon as we came, but nobody gave me the message. The butler didn't take it, but perhaps one of the officers did and forgot all about it in the excitement. She called again while you were in that other room with Taggert."

"Step on it, Shell," said Frieze. "Jimmy Knight was out at Sikkim's tonight, too."

"When?" asked Mr. Tinney.

"According to the butler, about eleven o'clock. He arrived right after Roche, that perfume association secretary, left. We put in a call to have Roche picked up and brought down to headquarters as soon as Payne, the butler, told us about him being there. I was going down from here, but I think I'll do better seeing Knight. Taggert's coming in to talk to Roche anyhow, and I can see him later."

He paused to light a cigarette, then went on, "Another thing: that Frangipanni you talked to last night, he's scrammed, too. Just breezed out without taking any of his clothes or anything. We've got more pickup orders out on this case than on a vice roundup."

"You won't have any trouble picking him up, Hank," said Mr. Tinney. "He's bandaged up like a mummy. By the way, did the butler hear any of the conversation, Hank? Either between Mr. Roche and Mr. Sikkim, or Jimmy and Mr. Sikkim?"

"No," said Frieze, "or if he did, he's not saying. Knight's going out there is another reason I think Ben might have killed his old man. I've thought right along that the old man engineered that picture of Knight and your Wills girl through Landry. With Landry dead, maybe Knight didn't get paid off and maybe he was coming out to collect from Sikkim. If Ben overheard Knight and his old man talking about that, I don't think he'd have hesitated a minute to stick a knife in the old man."

Mr. Tinney didn't answer, so I figured even he felt it looked pretty bad for Carol and Ben.

"What else came out in your questioning, Hank?" he asked finally.

"Nothing much. Right after Payne—that's the butler—let Knight in, Payne went up to bed. The servants' quarters are all the way over in the east wing of the house and none of them heard or saw anything after that. I'm inclined to believe them. Taggert does a good job with the hired help."

Frieze interrupted himself to light another cigarette before he told us the rest.

Mrs. Sikkim herself, it seemed, had discovered the body. She'd been unable to sleep and had walked to her bedroom window for a breath of air and had noticed this strange, bulky thing in the pool. She'd run down and found Sikkim. She'd called Kerwin, then Mr. Tinney. Mr. Kerwin, it seemed, was her best friend. He had called the Long Island cops.

When Frieze finished, Mr. Tinney said innocently, "I had quite a talk with Mrs. Sikkim tonight."

It's not that I'm smarter than Frieze. I just know Mr. Tinney better. I didn't bite. He did.

"Learn anything important?" he asked.

"Perhaps," said Mr. Tinney. "More than anything else, however, I verified my earlier conclusions about Amerandra Sikkim and particularly about Mrs. Sikkim's feelings toward him."

"You mean she *didn't* like him?" asked Frieze.

"He means," I put in, "that he was right again!"

"Shelley, just because you're tired is no reason why you should become nasty. We're all tired." He turned to Frieze, who was seated at his right. "She not only didn't like him, Hank, she hated him. And with good cause. He has been extremely cruel to her throughout their marriage. He was responsible, for instance, for the loss of her right arm."

Frieze sat up a little straighter. "How'd that happen? I've been curious about it."

"They were in an automobile accident. He was driving and lost control of the car and they smashed into a tree. This was in Lisbon in 1931. They were living there at the time. He escaped with minor injuries, but her arm was broken. At that, it would probably have been all right, but she was only in the hospital one day when he took her out.

"He wanted to leave Lisbon. He had an opportunity to buy in on a very well-established essential oil house in London and he wasn't going to pass it up. She wanted him to go on ahead, but he wouldn't hear of it. He was very jealous of her, it seems, very distrustful He forced her to leave the hospital and start out for London with him at once." Mr. Tinney shrugged his shoulders. "Gangrene set in and her arm had to be amputated."

"Seems to me," said Frieze, "she was a fool for going. He couldn't have done anything if she refused."

"She was, unquestionably," said Mr. Tinney, "but Sikkim was a man of strong will. He wielded an almost Svengalian influence on her for years before she learned to defend herself successfully. Mrs. Sikkim came from a very wealthy and a very fine family. She broke her parents' hearts when she married Sikkim. But she did. He was a fascinating man, still was even now, at—I should say, roughly—fifty-five. Twenty-five or thirty years ago he must have been quite a dashing and romantic figure. He was a graduate of Calcutta University at twenty, and when he met and married Katherine Boone—that was Mrs. Sikkim's maiden name—he'd traveled over half the world and was already well thought of in the field of perfume-chemistry. He reminds me a great deal of Enrique Frangipanni."

"If he kicked his wife around like that," said Frieze, "maybe she got fed up with it and murdered him."

"Hardly," said Mr. Tinney. "With a man of Mr. Sikkim's nature a woman like Mrs. Sikkim would have reached the point where she decided murder was the answer oh, say, ten years ago. She probably did reach that point and for one reason or another didn't do it. She's long since gone beyond that stage. She has successfully rebuilt her life, and has left him out of it almost entirely. Of course, they lived together, but hardly as man and wife in the true sense."

"I don't know," said Frieze. "Now that he's dead, chances are she'll come into a pretty big hunk of money."

"Hank, I'm surprised at you. Mrs. Sikkim probably has more money in her own right than Mr. Sikkim has been able to amass in almost three decades of ruthless operation. It was her money—left to her by her parents—which really started Mr. Sikkim on his career as a perfume tycoon."

"I'll go along with you on her innocence, at least for the time being," said Frieze, "for one reason above all others. There was another note. Taggert found it on Sikkim's body. I figure chances are the person who killed Sikkim also did for Landry. And as far as we've been able to find out up to now, Mrs. Sikkim had absolutely nothing to do with Landry."

"Have you got the note?" Mr. Tinney asked.

"Yeah. I had a hell of a time talking Taggert into letting me take it. I'm going to check the typing with the notes the boys in the lab are working on now." He took a sheet of paper out of his pocket and handed it to Mr. Tinney. "There's no perfume on this one."

Mr. Tinney sniffed. "Absolutely none," he confirmed, and read the note aloud.

THE ODOR IS GONE, AND SO YOU DIE.

I saw out of the corner of my eye that the slanted lines and the ovals and circles were the signature to this one, too.

"You think the water might have washed the perfume off this one?" I asked.

"I don't know," said Frieze. "I don't think so, but I guess it's possible. The lab men'll be able to tell."

"How are they progressing with their identification of the other notes?" asked Mr. Tinney.

Frieze shook his head. "Last time I checked they were absolutely stumped. They're still working on 'em, though, and they may hit it yet. They've called in a couple of perfumer-chemists, but it hasn't helped. Hurry it up, will you, Shell?"

I was already doing sixty-five, but I jammed the accelerator all the way down.

"Hey, what about the knife?" I asked, thinking of it all of a sudden. "Didn't they find it this time either?"

"No sign of it," said Frieze. "The uniformed men and Hanley, the guy with Taggert, put in some time looking for it before we got there. And you saw them starting all over again when we left."

"Of course they didn't find it, Shelley," said Mr. Tinney, getting a little irritable himself, "If they had, Captain Taggert would have been brandishing it all over the place."

I rolled off the Triborough Bridge at the 125th Street ramp and started downtown.

But dawn was beginning to wash the blackness out of the sky entirely before we made it down to Ninety-third and over to the West Side. I sure wanted to be in on the business with Jimmy, but when I thought of what Mamie was going to say to Frieze and me about keeping Mr. Tinney out all night, I almost lost my courage.

When Mr. Tinney caught up with us on top of the stoop, though, and quietly unlocked the door with his key and shoved the door open, I saw that Mamie wasn't going to say anything—not for a while, anyway. She lay in the small foyer with a nasty gash in the back of her head that still seeped blood slowly.

I knelt down beside her and Mr. Tinney said, "Get her onto that couch in the living room. Quickly, Shelley!"

He flattered me. I couldn't move Mamie single-handed any more than I could move the Empire State Building. I looked up for Frieze to ask him to give me a hand, but Frieze wasn't there. He'd run into the living room and now I saw him cross it and I heard his voice. He was calling Centre Street again.

He gave them the address, ordered up a bunch of detectives by name, told them to send along the meat wagon and Doc Kammerer. Then he came back into the foyer and helped me carry Mamie into the living room and over to the couch.

As he backed me in, I looked over my shoulder and saw Jimmy Knight. He was sprawled in front of the desk, with the back of his head and shoulders resting against it. Horror was in his eyes, though pain had twisted the expression out of the rest of his face. He'd been stabbed more than once, I guessed from the wet, red mess all over his chest and in his lap.

"Our killer's had an awful busy morning," said Frieze.

9

"Call Dr. Schwartz, Shelley," Mr. Tinney said, as he set about making Mamie as comfortable as possible. I did, and Frieze and Mr. Tinney started to look around. I turned from the phone in time to see Frieze pick up a wispy ball of cloth that someone had dropped near the desk.

"Our girl friend again," Frieze said, as he handed it to Mr. Tinney.

Mr. Tinney looked at the handkerchief. I moved closer and in the corner I saw the embroidered initials C.W. Frieze moved to the desk and carefully, in a handkerchief of his own, picked up a pad of yellow paper which Mr. Tinney used to make notes on the various cases he handled. The top sheet had been ripped off. A jagged piece of the top still remained. Frieze held the pad so that the light hit it at a certain angle.

"I think our murderer might have slipped here. The impression of whatever was written on the top sheet of this pad went through to this sheet. The boys in the lab ought to be able to bring it out fine."

Mr. Tinney was looking more troubled and thoughtful than I'd ever seen him look.

"What apparently happened," he said, "was that Jimmy came here to talk to me. Somehow the murderer learned

that he was coming here and followed him. Jimmy probably got in before the murderer could get to him. . . ." He
stopped talking suddenly and started toward the front door.

Frieze said, "Hey, where are you going?"

"Come along," said Mr. Tinney.

He went down the stoop and around to the alley at the
side of the house where the garbage cans are kept. Frieze
and I were right behind him.

At the mouth of the alley, Mr. Tinney pointed and said,
"There it is!"

He was pointing to a spot right beneath one of the living room windows. A wooden box had been placed on top
of one of the garbage cans. From this perch it was easy to
see that any man of average height could have looked right
into the living room.

"The killer watched Jimmy from there. When he saw
I wasn't home and Jimmy wasn't going to say anything to
Mamie, he just decided to wait. Then Jimmy probably got
fidgety waiting and asked Mamie for some paper. He started to write whatever he meant to tell me and the killer saw
him and decided he had to act."

"Don't be so sure of that 'he,'" said Frieze.

Mr. Tinney snorted. "Carol did not kill Mr. Landry
or Mr. Sikkim or Jimmy Knight. Just get that idea out
of your head, Hank. The killer came around to the front
door, rang the bell, probably hid behind the door when
Mamie opened it, and when Mamie came out to see who it
was, he struck her down and rushed into the living room
and stabbed Jimmy. Then he dragged Mamie's body inside
the foyer, shut the door and left."

"Sounds reasonable enough," Frieze commented.

"The impression on that pad should certainly tell us
something about it," said Mr. Tinney.

Mamie was coming around when we got back into the
house. She opened her eyes dazedly, saw Mr. Tinney and
said, "Mr. Tinney, are you all right?"

"Yes, yes, of course, Mamie. Are *you* all right?"

"I am," said Mamie, struggling to sit up, "but sure and I'd be a lot better if I could get my hands on the fiend who hit me." Then she turned and saw the body of Jimmy Knight. "Lord save us," she said, and made the sign of the cross.

We got her to talk finally and she told us what had happened. Mr. Tinney had hit it right on the head. Mamie didn't get a look at whoever hit her at all. He *had* hidden behind the door.

Sirens sounded as Mamie was finishing and Frieze walked to the door and the big parade started. Photographers, fingerprint men, Doctor Kammerer, the medical examiner, other homicide squad men. Doctor Schwartz showed up to take care of Mamie, who's a tough customer and hardly needed him. He patched her head and left.

Mr. Tinney, sure that Mamie was all right, sat quietly in a corner through it all with the fiercest frown of concentration on his face I'd ever seen there. He must have sat like that for an hour and a half. Finally he got up, looking actually cheerful, and came over to me.

"Shelley," he said, "would you drive me out to get some magazines? I'm much too excited to go to sleep. I'd like to read a little and relax my nerves."

There was a candy store just up the block, so I said, "I'll walk up the block and get you a couple. What do you want?"

"No," he said, "I don't want anything current. There's a very large second-hand magazine and book shop on Twenty-third Street and Sixth Avenue. I'd like to pick out something there."

"Do you feel all right?" I asked.

"Of course, Shelley," he said irritably. "However, if you don't choose to do me that little favor, just forget about it. I'll take a taxi."

I sat outside in the car, dozing, while he accepted the invitation on the big sign outside the second-hand shop to "Come in and Browse." I dozed maybe a half hour before he came out, his face beaming.

"All right, Shelley," he said.

There were two guys following him, each staggering under a burden of dirty-looking, dog-eared magazines. They must have been carrying fifty apiece. Mr. Tinney threw open the back door and said, "Just place them on the floor here, gentlemen."

I looked back at some of the titles: *True Detective Mysteries,* December 1925. *Startling Detective Adventures,* October 1926.

"What—" I started to say, as Mr. Tinney climbed in beside me.

"Detective stories." He spoke like a teacher explaining two and two to a backward child. "Detective stories of actual criminal cases."

"But you've got over a hundred of them and—"

"When you're studying a problem, Shelley, background is always invaluable."

I shrugged. I figured when you get as old as Mr. Tinney, it's only a question of time before your mind begins to crack. Besides, I was too tired and too hungry to care. I drove him back to the house where Frieze and his friends were just winding up.

As I staggered in with the second load of magazines, Frieze said, "What are those for?"

"Background," I said bitterly. "You don't know of any good correspondence schools for detectives, do you? I think Mr. Tinney would be interested."

"Shelley is just being nasty because he's tired, Hank," said Mr. Tinney. "Pay no attention to him."

Frieze's little helpers were filing out now with their various gadgets, but he slumped down in a chair and waited while Mamie came from the kitchen with a large glass of Mr. Tinney's vegetable juice.

Then Hank said, "The boys talked to Roche. It looks like he's in the clear. He was home in bed when they got there and his wife said he'd been home since a little after eleven-thirty. That's just about the time it would take him to get there from Sikkim's place."

"What were he and Mr. Sikkim talking about tonight?" asked Mr. Tinney.

"Some cockeyed new invention for making movies that smell," said Frieze.

"I've seen plenty of them that smelled without any inventions," I said.

"Quiet, Shelley," said Mr. Tinney. "What do you mean, Hank?"

"I don't know. Some guy's invented an electro-chemical process that sends out odors in the form of electrowaves, so if a dame's holding a bouquet of flowers in the picture on the screen, the audience smells it. What the hell's the difference?"

"None particularly," said Mr. Tinney. "It's very interesting."

"Roche is offering a reward of one thousand dollars on behalf of the association for information leading to the arrest and conviction of Sikkim's killer," said Frieze. "He says that Sikkim was one of the country's outstanding perfume men and a leading member of the association and—"

"That's interesting, too," said Mr. Tinney.

Frieze looked at him thoughtfully. "You know, Mr. Tinney, you look a lot more at ease and a lot more confident than at any time since you got into this. You aren't holding out on me, are you?"

"No, Hank, of course not. I've had a little time to think and I've formulated a few theories about these murders." He sipped at his juice.

"If there had been a previous attempt made on Mr. Sik-kim's life and the police had been called in, that could be checked, couldn't it?" he asked Frieze.

Surprise popped into Frieze's usually expressionless face. "Yeah," he said. "As a matter of fact, Kerwin told us about one such attempt. I didn't mention it before because Kerwin said the guy who tried to bump Sikkim died in a nuthouse about six months later. I wanted to check the records on it to make sure before I talked about it. How did you know?"

"I didn't really. It's just that such an attempt would have a logical place in one of my theories. It happened in the nineteen thirties, didn't it?"

Frieze was really sitting up and taking notice. Of course, Kerwin might possibly have told Mr. Tinney the same story he'd told Frieze, but I didn't think so, and I'm sure Frieze didn't either. Mr. Tinney is an egotist and a braggart, but I've never yet found him to lie to make himself seem smart.

"Yeah," said Frieze. "According to Kerwin, it happened in May of 1934. Sikkim was leaving his office one evening when this guy stepped out of the crowds walking along on the avenue and emptied a gun at him. Got him in the meaty part of the thigh with one bullet and missed him with the other five. It was only by the grace of God he didn't hit anybody else.

"The traffic cop on the corner of Fifty-seventh busted through and had to pretty near beat the guy's brains out to get him to come along. If he wasn't wacky before, he certainly was after that shellacking. Nobody could make any sense out of what he kept screaming after he regained consciousness. Kerwin says Sikkim denied ever having seen the guy before, but he pressed charges anyway. Assault and battery and attempted homicide. It didn't make much difference because the alienists said he was nuts and they put him away. Like I told you, Kerwin says he died six months later. I'm going to check it."

"Didn't Mrs. Sikkim tell you about the same case?" asked Mr. Tinney.

"She didn't know much about it. She was in England at the time."

"I see," said Mr. Tinney. "This man who attempted to kill Mr. Sikkim, what was his name?"

"Kerwin didn't recall," said Frieze. "He did say—"

"That the man was a Portuguese?" finished Mr. Tinney.

Frieze whipped around in his seat. "Yeah," he said. "You wouldn't be holding out on me, Mr. Tinney, would you? How do you know all about this?"

"Please, Hank, of course I wouldn't hold out on you. I have passed on to you every bit of information Shelley and I have picked up, haven't I, Shelley?"

"You have," I said. But I was beginning to feel nasty-tired again so I added pointedly, "As far as I know."

Mr. Tinney tried to scorch me with his eyes, but I pretended not to notice. He turned back to Frieze.

"Hank, you have my word that as soon as I am certain who murdered Noel Landry, Amerandra Sikkim and Jimmy Knight I will tell you. I will not make rash guesses, nor any definite statements as to who I believe the murderer is until I am quite sure that I am correct. Is that all right?"

"Yeah," said Frieze. "It'll have to be, I guess. In the meantime, I'll settle for Ben Sikkim and his girl friend and with any luck at all we ought to be able to pick them up pretty soon."

10

To sleep, I thought happily on the way over to my hotel on uptown Broadway. To sleep, perchance, to dream . . . dah, dah, dee, ah, dah!

But it didn't work out. I got into bed and sighed and closed my eyes. And then I began to try to figure out who murdered Landry and why. And who murdered Sikkim and why? And who murdered Knight and why? I certainly didn't want to, but there was nothing I could do about it. My body was weary and my mind was too, but my mind was also stubborn. It kept asking me questions.

Who was the mad Portuguese? What would the note Jimmy Knight was writing tell us? Where had Ben and Carol Wills disappeared to? What did the counterfeit perfume racket have to do with the murders? Or Frangipanni's aromatic petroleum refining formula? And where was Frangipanni? Who had sent the perfumed notes? Why hadn't he perfumed the last one, the one found on Sikkim? What was Landry doing with the list of perfume manufacturers, and did the little piece of rubber found on the floor beside Landry's bed mean anything? Who lived in the Jane Street apartment house that Landry was nosing around in? Did Mrs. Sikkim hate her husband enough to kill him? Or did her best friend, Randolph Kerwin? Or Ben? Or Carol Wills?

I finally convinced myself that I was never cut out to be a detective and I thought, well stupid, maybe now you'll go to sleep. But I didn't. I reminded myself that I was in the business of managing radio's foremost human relations counselor and how about that program? Wakely still wanted to see that script today. And Mr. Tinney still insisted that he was dropping the show. I got out of bed, walked over to the dresser and picked up my wristwatch. It was almost noon.

I got my *Leaves of Grass.* I figured if anybody can soothe me, can put me to sleep, Whitman can. I started to read his *Song of the Open Road,* but one of the stanzas reminded me of Mr. Tinney, so I skipped the rest of it and read through some others until I got to *Ashes of Soldiers.* I came to the lines,

> *Perfume therefore my chant, O love! immortal love!*
> *Give me to bathe the memories of all dead soldiers,*
> *Shroud them, embalm them, cover them all over with tender pride!*
> *Perfume all—make all . . .*

"Perfume, nuts!" I said and I wasn't sleepy at all any more. I closed Whitman and went and showered and dressed again.

I had a double steak dinner sent up and polished it off and then I felt better. I decided to work up a script for the program myself. I just made up the cases out of things I'd read and dreamed and bumped into here and there. I typed the final draft for Wakely, with a carbon for Catlett and Hall, the advertising agency.

Of course, I was hoping to sell Mr. Tinney the idea of doing the show before Tuesday rolled around. I figured

I would hire professional actors and actresses to be our clients. Certainly it was desperate stuff, but you just don't toss away fifteen hundred dollars a week without a struggle.

About three I got to Wakely's office.

"So you've finally talked Mr. Tinney into submitting a script," he said. "It's a good thing you did. We've had enough of his foolishness."

"It's going to be a terrific show," I said. "Read it."

He got to page eight before he commented.

"This one," he said, "about the girl who married her own brother and didn't know it; is it safe?"

"Certainly," I said, "we're not going to mention any names. The girl has expressed her desire to appear on the program. It's all set."

From Wakely's I went to the agency. William J. Catlett, president of the Catlett and Hall Advertising Agency, liked the script even better than Wakely. He was young, successful and exuberant.

"This is great, Shelley," he said, "but I have something to show you, too. We're working on our fall campaign and I've built the whole thing around Mr. Tinney. Come here, I'll show you."

He took me to a very large table against one wall of his huge office. It was piled high with boxes of Wakely Soap Chips, and giant-sized, leather-covered folders. He took one of the folders and stood it on the table, tent-fashion. He lifted the leather cover with *Wakely Soap Chips* embossed on it in fine gold letters, flipped it back out of sight, and revealed a comprehensive layout of a full-page advertisement in four colors. Even in the rough, the layout man had done a beautiful job on Mr. Tinney's face. His white hair glistened with dignity and there was the milk of human kindness in his blue eyes.

The portrait was set over a broad crimson panel with a black headline which said:

DESMOND TINNEY
The Man Who Has Solved
Thousands of Personal Problems
NOW SOLVES "EVERYWOMAN'S"
GREATEST PROBLEM
What to do about work-ugly hands

In the lower right-hand part of the advertisement was another panel, which featured a dramatic drawing of a woman reaching out her arms toward another woman, who was holding a little girl. "That's my baby, I tell you . . . that's my baby!" the woman without the child was screaming. Alongside the drawing the ad said, THE CASE OF THE MERRY MOTHER and beneath this:

A young mother, hungry for the bright lights, gaiety and glamour, deserts her baby. Another woman takes the child, rears her into blossoming girlhood. Six years later, the mother realizes the emptiness of the life she has led, finds the other woman, and demands the return of her child!

How would you solve this problem? Truly a case for a Solomon. But Desmond Tinney, Wakely Soap Chips' Human Relations Counselor, decided it to the complete satisfaction of both women, and in the best interests of the child.

This is only one of the many fascinating cases presented by Wakely Soap Chips every Tuesday evening in the hope of aiding a troubled humanity. Consult your local newspapers for time and station. Be sure to listen to Wakely Soap Chips'
HOUR OF DES TINNEY

On the other side was a picture of a red box of Wakely's Soap Chips.

I stared at the ad so long, Catlett finally said, "What's the matter, Shelley? You sick?"

I moved to a chair and sat down. "I've been getting these dizzy spells lately, Bill. I'll be all right in a minute."

Wakely Soap Chips' *Hour of Des Tinney!*

"Where did you get that line?" I asked Catlett.

"Which line?"

I pointed to it and read it aloud.

"Isn't it terrific?" he said joyously. "After all his name is Desmond Tinney, isn't it? And 'Des' is short for Desmond. And what does he do but practically decide the destiny of every person who comes to him for advice! I was working down here late one night and it hit me like a bolt of lightning. Isn't it a natural?"

"Yeah," I said feebly. "Yeah, it sure is." I got up and started for the door. "Bill, I'm late . . . I don't feel well . . . I should have been there an hour ago . . . I'll see you later."

After all, how much can a human being stand?

I went over to Mr. Tinney's.

I got up to the top of the stoop, when I saw the police car come down the street and pull up in front of the house. Frieze stepped out and joined me.

"You're not following *me* around now, are you?" I said. "I didn't murder anyone. Honest, I didn't."

"Shut up, Shell," Frieze said. "This isn't funny."

Mamie answered the door finally and said, "Oh, it's you two again. Why don't you go away and leave Mr. Tinney alone?"

"Is he in, Mamie?" Frieze asked wearily.

"No. He hasn't been to bed at all yet. He's been out all day. He stayed around and wrote a long letter after you left him this morning. Then he read those silly detective magazines. Then he went out to mail the letter and he hasn't come back since."

"Did he say where he was going?" asked Frieze.

"No. He just said he'd be back soon. That was nearly five hours ago."

Frieze shook his head. "I hope he hasn't got himself hurt," he said. "He's an awful old fool to go messing around with this kind of a murderer on the loose."

"He can take care of himself," I said, but I thought, God, I don't care if he never does another broadcast just so long as he's alive and well.

The door chime bonged and I raced to answer it.

It was Mr. Tinney, with a large envelope under his arm. "I forgot my keys, Shelley," he said. "Sorry to have to make you get up."

I scowled at him. "Why don't you let people know where you're going and when you're coming back?"

He smiled at me very pleasantly, and said, "Hello, Hank," as he came into the living room and saw Frieze.

"Where've you been all day?" asked Frieze.

"Busy," said Mr. Tinney, "very busy! I've talked to Mrs. Sikkim again, to Randolph Kerwin, and to Mr. and Mrs. Roche. I think we'll be solving these murders pretty soon now, Hank."

"I think," said Frieze, "we'll be solving them as soon as we lay our hands on young Ben Sikkim. Here," He handed Mr. Tinney a sheet of paper with typing on it. I moved over to Mr. Tinney's chair and read it.

Dear Mr. Tinney,
I doped Carol and fixed for Landry to get that picture of us. I didn't want to see the kid marry anybody else and Landry give me a hundred bucks and promised me four hundred more. But I don't want to see the kid take no murder rap.

I saw who killed Landry. It wasn't her. Her boy friend—

That's where Knight had stopped. Of all places. Mr. Tinney handed the paper back to Frieze.

"I assume this is taken from the impression on the pad. It's what Jimmy Knight was writing when he was killed."

"That's right."

"In my opinion," said Mr. Tinney, "it doesn't by any means prove that Ben killed Landry."

"It doesn't? It says very plainly, 'her boy friend . . .' That's Ben, isn't it?"

"Yes, but it's only the beginning of that sentence. Jimmy was apparently attacked before he could go any further. He might have meant to say that Carol's boy friend didn't kill Landry, either. Or that her boy friend did or did not do any one of a hundred other things."

"Nuts," said Frieze. "He's talking about the murder, isn't he?"

"Yes, but his mind was unquestionably in a very upset state. He wouldn't necessarily have been writing in a very logical and jointed manner. Chances, in fact, are against his writing that way."

"Well," Frieze said, "we still haven't been able to pick up Ben or the girl, but as soon as we do we'll know more about it."

"How about Frangipanni?" asked Mr. Tinney.

"He's still among the missing, too."

"I had quite a chat with Mr. Kerwin about him," said Mr. Tinney. "He came to Siquin very highly recommended. As a matter of fact, he is supposed to be a direct descendant of the famous Marquis Frangipanni who invented the method of perfuming gloves."

"How very dull," I said.

"Quiet, Shelley," Mr. Tinney said. "By the way. Hank, did you check on the death of that Portuguese who tried to kill Sikkim in 1934?"

"Yeah. His name was Savoldi. He died in the Mattamore Home for the Insane on December eighth that same year. His heart gave out."

Mr. Tinney nodded and said to Mamie, who was passing by, "Mamie, please bring me some juice and some coffee for Mr. Frieze and Shelley."

"By the way," Frieze said, "we did find out one other, interesting thing. The super of that Jane Street apartment identified Sikkim, Senior, as the guy who rented it from him. Sikkim was a pretty gay dog, the way the super tells it. Used to bring all kinds of gals down there. Blondes, redheads, brunettes, all kinds. The only thing they had in common was they were all lookers."

Mamie brought in Mr. Tinney's juice. "I'll be having the coffee along in a minute," she said in a voice that indicated a distinct possibility that she might put arsenic in it.

"We checked that last note, too," Frieze went on, "the one we found on Sikkim. I think it was a phony. It wasn't even written on the same typewriter as the other four. What did pick up today, Mr. Tinney? Anything that might help?"

"Oh, I don't 'know," said Mr. Tinney. "I ran into a girl friend of Shelley's. . . ."

"You did?" I said.

"Yes. Remember that *Morning's Laughter* portrait in the ground floor window of Siquin's? That lovely looking Irish girl you were admiring so much?"

"Yeah." I felt relieved. "What about her?"

"She's Mrs. Roche. Interesting, isn't it?" Mr. Tinney grinned at us. "I also stopped at Siquin's advertising agents and picked up proofs of their entire campaign for the last season, and this."

Frieze looked puzzled. "What for?" he inquired.

"I was just curious. Would you like to see them?"

He walked over to the desk and brought over the large envelope he'd carried when he came in. He took out a mass of glossy proofs of perfume advertisements. Frieze and I looked through them and handed them back to him.

Frieze asked, "What's all this got to do with these murders?"

"Maybe nothing and maybe something," said Mr. Tinney. "I want to call your attention specifically to the fact that that very lovely portrait of Mrs. Roche which expresses the mood of *Morning's Laughter* so appropriately is not used in any of the *Morning's Laughter* advertisements."

Frieze said, "You're way over my head. Suppose it wasn't used, what does that prove?"

Mr. Tinney shrugged. Even Frieze was getting slightly annoyed.

"Would you mind explaining what you think it *might* mean?" he asked a little irritably.

"Yes, I would," said Mr. Tinney, "because it may mean nothing at all. Here's your coffee."

Frieze picked up his cup, sipped the top off and said, "You didn't learn anything else interesting, did you?" There was just the slightest trace of sarcasm in his voice.

"Yes," said Mr. Tinney. "Mr. Roche still wears shirts that are too large for him."

Frieze sighed, meaning, "I give up."

"By the way, gentlemen," said Mr. Tinney, "I'm leaving town tomorrow morning."

"Where are you going?" asked Frieze.

"Just on a little trip."

"What about the broadcast?" I said. "Will you be back in time to do it?"

"I told you, Shelley, as far as I'm concerned there aren't going to be any more broadcasts."

"Does your trip have something to do with these kill-ings?" asked Frieze.

"Possibly. I can't tell right now."

Frieze got up. "Well, have a good trip," he said. He left. I think he was a little glad that Mr. Tinney was leaving. He'd looked for some real help from the old gent and so far he'd certainly gotten a lot of anything but that.

Mamie stalked out from the kitchen. "Shelley," she said, "why don't you go home so that Mr. Tinney can get some sleep? You'll have the poor old gentleman killing himself over these terrible crimes."

"*I'll* have him killing himself!" I screamed. "Me! I'd kiss even you, Mamie, if you could get him to forget about them and go back to nice sane problems."

"Children! Children!" admonished Mr. Tinney with an evil and enigmatic smile.

I hung around for a couple of hours trying to talk him out of the trip, which he refused to tell me anything about, and into doing the broadcast. The best I could get was his promise that maybe if he got back in time he'd do the show, if I behaved and if the murders were cleared up by then.

"Two very good friends of ours, Carol Wills and young Ben Sikkim, are in grave danger of being caught and convicted for these murders," he said. "Until we get them out of this mess, we can't think about anything else."

And the next morning he left on his trip. And I'll bet if he knew what was going to pop that day, he never would have gone. Ben and Carol were damn near killed themselves.

11

I'd hustled around all of that next morning, lining up and rehearsing the actors for the show, which if worst came to worst I was going to do myself. I was back in my hotel room with them when the phone rang. I picked it up and barked "Hello." Mrs. Sikkim said "Hello" back at me, and there was the same nervous tension in her voice that there had been the time she'd called Mr. Tinney about Sikkim's death.

"Mr. Shell," she said, "I've got to see you right away."

"Where are you?" I asked.

"Down in the lobby."

"C'mon up," I said.

I shooed the actors and actresses out of the room with some fast instructions about where and when to meet me the next day. Mrs. Sikkim pushed in before the last of them were gone. Randolph Kerwin was with her.

"What's the matter, Mrs. Sikkim?" I asked, closing the door behind them.

"It's Ben and Carol. They've had an accident. The—the car crashed. They're in a hospital in Pennsylvania. Where can I reach Mr. Tinney? I want him with me. I—I—"

"He's gone out of town," I said. "And he didn't tell anyone where he was going. Maybe I can help."

"Oh, yes . . . please. Will you come?"

Why either she or I should have thought I could help I don't know, but anyway I was willing to try.

"Sure," I said. "Let's go."

We went down and got into Kerwin's car, a big, black, high-powered job. He drove and Mrs. Sikkim sat up in front with him and I sat in the back.

"They're not seriously hurt, I hope," I said.

"I don't know," she replied. "Captain Frieze just called me. He said they were all right, but—but he wouldn't tell me anything else even if they weren't."

When I say Kerwin drove I mean just that. I thought I was pretty good with a car myself, but he made that job do everything but talk. We made it to Holicong, Pennsylvania, in an hour and three-quarters. The hospital was about a half mile out from there and we made that in less than a minute.

We went right to the desk and Mrs. Sikkim asked for Ben's room.

"Oh, I'm afraid you won't be able to go up for a while yet," said the reception nurse. "There's a gentleman up there with him now."

"But I'm his mother."

"I'm sorry, madam," the nurse said, "I can't allow more than one person at a time to visit Mr. Sikkim."

"Who's with him now?" asked Randolph Kerwin.

"A Captain Taggert," said the girl, "from the New York Police Department."

"Where's his doctor?" demanded Kerwin angrily. "What are they trying to do, kill the boy?"

Just then Frieze and a short, stocky man in a blue business suit and two uniformed Pennsylvania State Troopers came through the swinging doors at one end of the marble-tiled floor. We hurried over to them.

"They're all right, Mrs. Sikkim," Frieze said, "I don't know how they missed getting killed, but Ben just busted a couple of ribs, and they've got him strapped up and he's feeling pretty good now. The girl is just suffering from nervous shock. She'll be all right before morning.

"What is Taggert doing up in his room?" Kerwin asked.

Frieze shrugged his shoulders. "You know Taggert," he said. "I tried to get him to wait until morning, but he wouldn't. The doctor—oh, this is Doctor Schmidt, Mrs. Sikkim; the boy's mother, Doctor, and Mr. Kerwin and Mr. Shell. Doctor Schmidt felt it would be all right if Taggert talked to him for just a moment. Under the circumstances I couldn't stop him."

"Under what circumstances?" Kerwin was abrupt. "That boy wasn't well when he left New York. After an accident like this, he certainly shouldn't be—"

"That's just it," said Frieze. "It wasn't just a plain accident. They ran off the road and turned the car clean over taking a turn. They were trying to get away from these officers."

Mrs. Sikkim said, "Oh, my God, my God. . . ."

Frieze turned to the doctor. "Suppose I take Mrs. Sikkim upstairs, Doc, and get Taggert out of there. After all, the boy's mother ought to—"

"By all means, Captain," said Doctor Schmidt. "I'm sorry, madam, about Captain Taggert, but he said the boy was wanted for—for murder. I had to let him up."

Kerwin clasped Mrs. Sikkim's hand. "Keep your chin up, Katherine. Everything will be all right."

He let go of her hand and Frieze led her to the elevator. The doctor and the two state highway cops moved off and Randolph Kerwin raged. "When I lay my hands on that Taggert, I'll—"

"Take it easy, Mr. Kerwin," I said. "He's just a very stupid guy trying to do a job."

Taggert came down with Frieze shortly after Mrs. Sikkim left Kerwin and me standing in the hospital lobby. Kerwin walked toward them as they got out of the elevator.

"Listen, Taggert," he said tightly, "I want you to understand that this is the twentieth century, not the Inquisition. You can't—"

Taggert scowled down at him belligerently. "What's eatin' you?"

"You could have waited until morning to talk to that boy."

"Waited, hell! He cracked up running from the state cops and he wasn't just worried about getting a speeding ticket. As soon as we can move him, I'm taking him back to New York and he's going to talk."

Frieze said, "You'll have plenty of chance to talk to him from now on, Taggert. He's not running away, the shape he's in."

"Damn right, I will," Taggert bellowed, "and there's something I want to tell you, Mr. Kerwin. You're not in the clear yourself yet on this thing. The whole business is being left to you. You made plenty on Sikkim's death."

Kerwin drew back his right and tore at Taggert. But Frieze grabbed him and said, "Take it easy, Mr. Kerwin."

Taggert laughed nastily and walked away from us and out of the hospital. Frieze held onto Kerwin while he quieted.

"There's no use getting all steamed up, Mr. Kerwin," he said. "I'm not saying Taggert's right, but those two kids sure did everything possible to make it look bad for themselves. I talked to Miss Wills and she admits that when the boy met her at the prison it was about one o'clock. He could easily have killed his father and then gone on into town for her. I wouldn't even be surprised if he did."

"It's ridiculous," Kerwin exploded.

"Maybe," said Frieze, "but the kid won't even deny that he killed his father. Just keeps saying he's glad the old man's dead and that's all. I know he's been in pretty bad mental shape lately, but, even so, talk like that isn't doing him any good."

"The boy isn't responsible for what he's saying," insisted Kerwin.

Frieze shrugged. "Maybe not. But he's not helping himself and the girl hasn't helped any, either. She admits going to Mr. Tinney's the night Sikkim and her ex-husband were killed. She took Ben to a girl friend of hers in town and she went up to Mr. Tinney's to get his help, she says. When she saw Mamie and Knight she got scared again and went back to Ben. By that time she couldn't hold him any longer. She was scared to death because he looked wild, like he might do something desperate. So she went with him. He drove and drove and rambled on like a lunatic about how his old man wasn't going to run his life any more. He drove half the night, till she finally got him to stop at a tourist camp. And the rest of the night he raved, half asleep and half awake, about all kinds of crazy things."

"Listen, Captain," I said, "you saw him at Sikkim's yourself Wednesday. You saw the condition he was in."

"I know, I know," said Frieze, "but it looks bad for those kids, no matter what you say."

He took out a pack of cigarettes and passed them and we each took one and lit up. Three on a match. None of us were superstitious.

"I'll have to take the girl back tomorrow morning myself," he said. "She's wanted for the Landry murder and maybe the Knight murder—and there's nothing I can do."

"Will she be in any shape to travel?" I asked.

"Yeah," said Frieze, "she just got a bad shaking up."

Mrs. Sikkim came out of the elevator and Kerwin hurried over to her.

Frieze looked at her and murmured, "Why the hell did I ever become a detective? It's the lousiest business in the world. Look at that woman. . . ."

I did and I knew Frieze was right. Of course, Mrs. Sikkim had looked worried and tired when she'd gone up and actually there wasn't much change. Just little things: the glazed pain spread over her eyes like tears of agony that had been smeared out thin and frozen; the way the corners of her mouth were pulled back and down; the sound of her voice, cold and beaten.

"I saw them both," she was saying as she came near us. "They're so—hurt and—and bewildered. They're— I can't, Randolph, I can't let them suffer like this. . . . I—"

Kerwin was holding her arm firmly and saying, "I know, Katherine. We'll get them out of this. We won't let them—"

"Look, Mrs. Sikkim," Frieze said, "the car was wrecked completely. But they were lucky. They'll both be all right. They weren't even seriously hurt. They—they— Hell!" He cut off abruptly. "Don't worry so much!" He stormed out of the hospital like he was mad at Mrs. Sikkim and Kerwin and me and the whole world.

There, I thought, goes a crazy and wonderful cop.

I drove to the hotel with Mrs. Sikkim and Kerwin and none of us said anything, but before we even got there I knew I wasn't staying over. You can stand around and watch people getting their hearts torn out just so long. Then you've got to get away from there. I took the next train back to town.

Half the night I lay awake wishing that if Ben or the girl didn't kill Landry and Sikkim and Knight, whoever did would come around and say so. The other half he did. Only he wasn't anybody I'd ever known. He had a green face and red eyes. If he looked like anybody at all, he looked like Boris Karloff in technicolor. He kept leering and saying, "Why, yes, Shelley dear, of course I murdered the gentlemen." It was a hell of a dream. I didn't wake up till eleven o'clock.

I took a shower and dressed and still felt awful, so I went down and had some orange juice and coffee and that didn't help, so I called Mr. Tinney.

Mamie answered. "No, he hasn't come back yet, Shelley, and why don't you take those long tiresome trips and let an old gentleman like Mr. Tinney have his normal life? You ought to be good for something!"

She was going to say some more but I put the receiver back on the hook and thought maybe if I did some work, I'd be able to get my mind off the murder. So I rounded up my actors and actresses and spent the rest of the day rehearsing them again. I began to think the show would be pretty good even if Mr. Tinney didn't come back in time.

I was a fairly happy man all that day and the next. Or at least the beginning of the next. Then I saw the Sunday papers. Benabala Sikkim inherited every penny his father had ever made and Mrs. Sikkim nothing, although she didn't need it anyway.

Carol Wills had been jugged again in New York and Ben was also in New York in the prison hospital. Murder charges were being filed against him immediately. Taggert had said he was going to solve the case within twenty-four hours and he had. Frieze said nothing. Frangipanni was still among the missing. The perfumed notes hadn't been successfully analyzed. The murder weapons hadn't been found.

Taggert, I gathered by reading between the lines, was still going heavy on the strong-arm stuff and Mrs. Sikkim was on the point of a nervous collapse herself.

I tossed the papers aside and finished my ham and eggs and called Mr. Tinney. Mamie told me, a little forlornly, that he hadn't come back yet. I wondered again where he had gone and why. And whether whoever he was chasing might not have stopped long enough to let the old gent catch him.

I continued to call Mamie all day Sunday, about once every half-hour. I listened to more Gaelic insults than I'd ever heard in my life. So far as Mamie was concerned, the whole thing was my fault, and as the hours passed and she became more and more anxious about Mr. Tinney, her barbs became nastier and Irisher. About eight that evening she was tossing 'em at me straight from Killarney. I was getting kind of anxious about Mr. Tinney myself. I called the Pennsylvania Railroad, and the New York Central and the B. & O. and the bus companies, trying to trace down whether or not Mr. Tinney had made a reservation on any of them. I had no luck at all.

About midnight I was still calling Mamie with no results. I went down to the Hotel Barworth's Iranian Room, where Lis Matthews, a gal singer I'd once managed, was appearing with the Teddy Sharon orchestra. That didn't do any good either.

Monday I went through the Sunday routine with variations. I called up everybody connected with the case. I called Mamie over and over and over again. No Mr. Tinney. If you were holding AT&T stock, those extra dividends were my doing. I finally went to bed and tossed, got up, read poetry and tossed some more.

And then it was Tuesday, the day of the broadcast. The idea of doing the show myself scared me plenty, but I'd still do it to save that fifteen hundred a week.

I got on the phone and rounded up my actors and actresses and ran through a final rehearsal. That took the morning and part of the afternoon. A couple of hours before show time I went over to Mr. Tinney's. I was still hoping he'd show up. And I didn't even care if he wouldn't do the show just so long as he'd turn up—without a knife wound.

The phone rang and I leaped for it. It was Frieze.

"Is Mr. Tinney there, Shell?" he asked.

"No."

"Hell," said Frieze, "we picked up Frangipanni. He's a wreck. He's been hiding out in a fleabag down on the Bowery ever since he walked out that night. Taggert's been working him over and I've been trying to talk to him, but he won't give. I thought Mr. Tinney might come down and see what—"

"He's not back," I said again, "and when he does come back, I'm sitting on him until nine o'clock when he goes on the air. He can talk to Frangipanni or anybody else you've got after that."

"Have him call me down here at headquarters if he shows, will you, Shell? This greaser is stubborner'n all hell."

"I'll have him call you," I said, "if he comes back."

I hung up and paced some more.

A half-hour later the chimes rang and I thought maybe he forgot his key again—maybe this is him. But it wasn't. It was a special mail carrier with a big package that he wanted me to sign for. The package was addressed to Mr. Tinney in a flourishing, old-world handwriting and it had enough fancy stamps on it to start a collection. From the markings on it, I saw that it had come from Lisbon, Portugal, via Transatlantic Clipper.

Eight o'clock came and so did some of my actors and actresses, but no Mr. Tinney. By eight-thirty all but two of the cast had arrived and when the chimes sounded again, I didn't have much hope. Just another actor, I thought. But it was Mrs. Sikkim. She looked so bad I stopped worrying about Mr. Tinney and the program.

"What's the matter, Mrs. Sikkim?"

"Is Mr. Tinney in, Mr. Shell? I *must* see him right away."

Her voice still had that beaten sound to it, but now it had something else too—a desperation, like the voice of a woman standing on the edge of a roof, saying goodbye.

"I'm sorry, Mrs. Sikkim," I said. "He's out of town. He hasn't come back yet."

"What—what about his program? Isn't it to be broadcast tonight?" she asked, and the look in her eyes matched her voice.

I stared at her. Why should she be worrying about Mr. Tinney's radio program?

"His program?" I repeated stupidly.

"Yes, yes. I want to—to speak over the air. I want to tell my—my story."

There are many nights since that I haven't been able to sleep because of what I did then. Maybe I went insane myself temporarily. Maybe it's the cold-blooded showman in me. Whatever it was, I said, "I'm afraid Mr. Tinney won't be back, Mrs. Sikkim. I'm going to do the show tonight. I'll be glad to have you speak if you want to."

I didn't know why she wanted to go on or what she was going to say, but I knew it was going to be like cutting pieces out of her soul. One part of me didn't want her to, wanted to stop her, but another part of me was saying, "What a show this'll make! They'll be talking about it for months."

"I do want to, Mr. Shell," she said. "I will be grateful to you if you can arrange it."

12

We didn't play to audiences. The balcony looking down into the studio was deserted. In the control booth sat two technicians. One fiddled with the instrument panel and the other stared evenly at the watch on the top of his wrist. In the thickly carpeted, sound-proofed studio I sat at a long, highly polished table with Mrs. Sikkim in another chair beside me. There were microphones on the table in front of each of us. There was a floor mike with the show's announcer behind it and a ceiling mike over the head of the show's organist. The rest of the show's cast sat in folding chairs along the side walls.

I looked at Mrs. Sikkim. A little trickle of liquid red moved slowly across her lower lip where her teeth were biting into it. I saw the control man signal the announcer. We were on the air.

The organ started to peal, a muted, deep-throated sound. At the table, the announcer's voice was little more than a whisper.

"Ladies and gentlemen, good evening. Wakely Soap Chips presents an hour with Mr. Desmond Tinney, counselor to the sore of heart, the man who has solved the problems of thousands of troubled men and women.

"Mr. Tinney, however, was unavoidably delayed in reaching the studio tonight. He is expected momentarily.

In the meantime, his friend and associate, Stanley Shell, will hear the first of tonight's cases.

"But before we proceed, ladies and gentlemen, just one more word. The makers of Wakely Soap Chips—the soap chips favored by millions of women everywhere because they make every washing task more pleasant, easier—bring you this program in the hope that you will profit by the mistakes of others, by the errors of these people whose problems are presented here.

"And now, ladies and gentlemen, Mr. Desmond Tinney's friend and associate, Stanley Shell."

I leaned forward and cast my eyes down at the script on the table before me. I said, a little shakily, "Before we begin, ladies and gentlemen, I want to make it clear . . ."

Miraculously my knees stopped quivering and my voice steadied. I disregarded the prepared script.

". . . I want to make it clear that Mr. Tinney was kept from this microphone tonight by the only thing short of death which could keep him from it. He is at the moment engaged in the investigation of certain circumstances which have a direct bearing on the very serious problem of the first lady who will speak to you tonight. In keeping with the policy of this program to protect those who come to it for counsel, I will not divulge this lady's name. I introduce her to you merely as Mrs. X-53414."

I nodded toward Mrs. Sikkim. She clutched the table's edge with her hand.

"I do not want anonymity," she said in a tense, vibrant voice. "People of this city, I want you to know who I am. I want you to help me. My name is Katherine Sikkim. Thursday morning my husband was murdered. I want to tell you about my husband and about myself."

She paused and was silent for a full moment. I half expected the studio to blow up with the air of electric excitement she had generated. The pause seemed to have helped her. She was calmer, somehow, but her face held a grim and earnest expression.

"I was a very young girl when I met him—it was my eighteenth birthday. I was a pampered girl, the only child of a quite wealthy family. I wanted to be an artist and I had forced my father and mother to let me go to Paris alone, in a time when girls of my age hardly dared go to a neighbor's house unescorted.

"I was in Paris when I met him and I loved life and all the wonderful adventures it promised. He was brilliant and handsome and had lived in the strange corners of the world about which I had dreamed. He came from a high-caste Brahman family from Calcutta. To me he was the embodiment of all the dashing heroes of history. He had already received his engineering degree from an Indian university and spoke English and his native tongue and several other languages well. He was the most fascinating person I had ever met."

She paused again and took a deep breath and spoke into the microphone with her eyes half closed.

"I want to tell you all of my story because I want you to understand what can happen to a girl's heart and—and soul to—to make her—

"Two months after we met we were married. In Paris. My husband was ambitious but I liked that. I was ambitious, too. He was ambitious to make money. He knew my family was wealthy, yes, but he worked harder than the poorest man.

"His ambition did not worry me. I admired it. But my ambition bothered him. He scoffed at my painting and said it was childish and that my duty was to be a good wife to him and nothing more. I tried to laugh him out of it, but as young as I was, I realized it was going to be difficult. Perhaps it would have worked out. Perhaps, after a time, I would have been glad to give up my painting—if he had been to me what he wished me to be to him.

"Shortly after our marriage, as shortly as two months after, certain friends of mine tried to warn me that my husband was seeing other women. I refused to believe them. And when they persisted in their stories, I stopped seeing them.

"I had implicit faith in my husband—the same faith I wished him to have in me. A half year after our marriage, an importer of civet and other perfumery materials in Paris told my husband of a position in Abyssinia which paid a rather high salary. It was on a farm in the interior where they raised civet cats. My husband accepted the position eagerly. And I was just as eager that he should. Abyssinia then sounded to me like a land of mystery and adventure. I didn't know about the heat and the dirt and filth and— and . . ." She closed her eyes fully now and gripped the tabled edge more tightly.

". . . or maybe I wouldn't have cared about all those things. Maybe they would have been as glamorous and exciting as I expected them to be . . . if what happened had not happened.

"We were there less than a week, when I came into our bedroom one evening and found my husband there with—with a native girl. I walked out of that room with something inside me dead. So dead that it has never come back. I packed my things and left, but before I got very far my husband caught me. It was just outside the town. It was hot and dark and there was a foul odor in the air. He forced my wagon to a stop and pulled me out of it and— and he beat me.

"The native drivers of my wagon and of his stood by chatting and as I sank into unconsciousness, with my whole body one tremendous lump of agony. I heard my husband's harsh breathing and the chatter of the drivers. I heard that rasping breath and that quiet, steady chatter in my dreams through many tortured days and nights while I lay in bed recovering. I hoped that the beating had done one thing. I hoped it had killed the baby which was stirring inside me. I prayed that it had killed the baby . . . and I prayed that I would die."

Her eyes closed tight, but not tight enough to keep the tears from squeezing out and moving slowly down her cheeks. I wondered if I ought to stop her. I wanted to, but I couldn't. She spoke faster now, as though she wanted to get it over with.

"I wanted to die worse than I ever wanted anything in all my life. But I didn't. And my baby didn't. He was born sickly and frail, but he lived. And I wanted to live once again myself.

"I didn't want to live with my husband, but I couldn't return to my parents' home. I hadn't even told them about my marriage until after it was all over. I didn't want to admit to them that I had made a mistake. I was young and very—very foolish and proud.

"So I stayed for a time. And there were other native girls. And more beatings . . . and I ran away many times. . . but my husband always found me and brought me back. We moved, but from one hell to another. From Abyssinia to Somaliland. From Somaliland to Tibet. My husband was still ambitious. He was grounding himself in perfume essentials: civet and tonquin musk and olibanum and evil-smelling fats and liquids. And this was my son's infancy, his boyhood: sickening odors and strange, cheap women visiting his home; the screams of his father that he was the master of his household and could do no wrong.

"As the years passed my husband flaunted his companions before me less and less. I had stopped caring and he

got no further satisfaction from it. And our son was grow-
ing older and—and my husband did love the boy, in his
own strange way.

"I tried to rebuild my life around my son and painting,
which I had once loved so much. I wasn't happy . . . I do
not think I will ever be happy again . . . but I was almost
contented. Then we moved to Lisbon. My husband had
bought a perfume distillery there. But he spent a great
deal of time in Madrid. He was away and had been for
three days. I had spent the afternoon painting a field of
tuberoses in full bloom. In the evening I sat at my easel,
touching up the oil painting I had started that afternoon.
Ben, my son, sat across the room, reading a book. My husband came in and I saw immediately that he was in a vile
mood. I went on with my painting, but the boy spoke to
him, something about the story he had been reading. He
began to scold the child and after a moment slapped him
so viciously that the boy fell in a heap against the chair on
which I sat.

"I got up and knelt beside my son and tried to soothe
him. My husband pulled me up and struck me. I rushed
at him and he knocked me to the floor. He saw the painting then and screamed that if I gave more attention to my
child and less to that stupid painting the boy wouldn't
be such an unbearable youth. I raged back at him and he
knocked me down again and in a fit of insane anger such
as I have never seen in a human being before or since, he
trampled my right hand with his foot. He must have kept
stamping on my hand even after I fainted from the excru-
ciating agony of it. I awoke in a hospital . . . and the next
day he demanded that I be dressed and come along with
him to London. He was leaving Lisbon for good.

"I fought him and the doctors fought him, but in the
end he had his way, as usual. Two days later in London I
had my right arm amputated. Gangrene had set in and it

was the only way the doctors could save my life. We stayed in London three months and then came to America.

"I told my mother and father that I had lost my arm in an automobile accident. I never breathed a word to them about the things which had happened to me in the years since I had been married. I tried to make them believe that I had been and was a happy wife. But they knew. At least, my mother knew. She died less than six months after my return. I don't know that she died of heartbreak and of a sense of failure in what she might have felt was her duty to me. I don't know that, but I believe it to be true. My father died a year, almost to the day, after my mother."

She paused again. Her cheeks were wet now and she was still holding the edge of the table. One of the actresses was making loud, sobbing sounds and others were sniffing and had handkerchiefs in their hands. I looked back at Mrs. Sikkim. Her eyes were open, and there was pure, unadulterated venom in them when she spoke again.

"I hated my husband as no human being has ever hated another. I asked him for a divorce. I pleaded with him to release me. But he refused. So once again I resigned myself to working out my life as best I could. I still had my son.

"In the past ten years, I did find a certain measure of contentment. I made friends here in this country who have helped more than I can say to erase the memory of the—of what had gone before."

She'd used the plural, but I knew somehow that she meant Randolph Kerwin.

"My son," she said, "and his father got along as well as could be expected with the shadow that existed, and would always exist, between them. They got along fairly well until a year ago when my son fell in love with a very sweet girl, a girl I would be proud to have for a daughter. At first my husband said nothing, but after a time he began to object violently to my son's association with this girl.

I have my own ideas about the reasons for his objections, ideas which I need not mention here. He would hear nothing of my son's desire to marry this girl. He threatened to disown the boy if he married her. I had sufficient money in my own right to amply take care of the boy's needs. But he didn't want my money, nor his father's. And knowing my husband as I did, I dared not interfere.

"Last Wednesday, the day before my husband was murdered, he made some vile remarks about the girl and my son heard him. They had a violent argument. They almost came to blows and my son, in the presence of a number of witnesses, among whom was a police officer, threatened to kill his father.

"The boy was on the verge of a nervous collapse. He did not know what he was saying. We managed to get him up to his room and to bed and called a doctor. The doctor prescribed complete rest, but early Thursday morning my son took the girl he loved out of prison, where she was being held in connection with another murder, and they fled. My son had a wild, half hysterical idea that there was only one thing left for him to do—to run away with the girl and marry her. The girl was too frightened to refuse.

"When my husband was murdered the police immediately suspected my son. They started a search for them, but did not find them until yesterday afternoon, when my son overturned the car in which he and the girl were driving. They were speeding to get away from two state patrolmen who were in pursuit.

"Despite the condition of the girl and my boy, the police, and one policeman in particular—a Captain Taggert—persisted in questioning and grilling them.

"I pleaded with him; I begged him to leave those two children alone until they had had at least a slight chance to recover from the trying experiences they have been through. Captain Taggert refused to listen!

"And so, this evening, less than an hour ago, I told Captain Taggert and his associates the truth. I told them I had killed my husband. I told them just how and why. I want to tell you . . . I want to tell you because I cannot stand to see my boy and that lovely, innocent child, who loves him as I do, suffer any longer.

"I want to tell you because Captain Taggert refuses to believe that I killed my husband. He says I have no motive. I told him how intensely I hated my husband, but he insists that is not motive enough. He has no evidence against me and he has evidence—circumstantial as it may be—again my son and the girl. I told Captain Taggert, in the presence of several newspapermen, that I killed my husband and even if he refused to arrest me, I would not be here talking to you tonight—if the newspapers would only print my story. But I'm afraid they will not. A very dear friend of mine who was also present when I confessed the murder told them that he would sue them into bankruptcy if they dared print one word of what I said. He made them believe that I was talking hysterically, that I was not in my right senses, that I was trying to protect my son against police brutality.

"I want to tell you people who are listening to me to protest, in the name of humanity, against any further persecution of my son and the girl. I want to convince you that I killed my husband. I want to tell you how and why. . . ."

She paused again and the sounds of quick breathing and sobbing and crying in the studio stilled, waiting for her to go on.

"Early Thursday morning," she said, "I was awakened by a noise, the sound of my husband coming down the hall. I heard him stop. I opened my door and saw him standing before my son's door. I came out and told him that the boy was sick. I asked him to leave him alone. He insisted that he had to talk to the boy. We argued and he finally went downstairs and out of the house. From my window, I saw him walking near the pool.

"I knew he would come back and waken Ben and I was worried about my son. I can't tell you how near the breaking point he was that afternoon during the argument. It came over me in a desperate, nauseating wave that as long as my husband was alive neither my son nor I could ever have a life of peace, much less one of happiness. For myself I didn't care, but I wanted my son to have more out of his life than I had had.

"Very cold-bloodedly, very deliberately, I made up my mind to kill my husband. I took a letter opener from my desk. I held it beneath the folds of my robe and I went downstairs and to my husband, who was still pacing up and down alongside the swimming pool.

"I may be a woman and I may not have great strength but I studied anatomy as part of my art training for a number of years. I know where every bone, every muscle in the human body is located. I faced my husband and talked to him. I was standing close, seeking out the exact spot, measuring the distance furtively with my eyes. I stabbed just once, quickly. I did not miss. I knew as soon as the blade touched him that I had pierced his heart.

"I pushed his body over into the swimming pool and went back into the house. I—"

What made me interrupt to ask it, I don't know. Maybe it was just unconscious imitation of the manner in which Mr. Tinney had handled a similar situation. I don't know what it was. All I know is that I didn't believe she murdered Sikkim. I didn't want to believe it. And I wanted to prove she didn't.

I said, "What did you do with the letter opener, Mrs. Sikkim?"

She turned and stared at me with a look in her eyes that turned my blood to ice. "The—the letter opener?"

she stammered, and laughed a sharp, high-pitched laugh. She kept on laughing and screamed between gasps of the insane sound. "The letter opener? That's why the police won't believe me . . . that's why the newspapers won't print my—my story. I can't tell you what I did with . . . the letter opener."

She laughed some more, crazier and crazier, and then in the middle of it toppled over sidewards off the chair. She toppled my way and I caught her. The studio became a riot of screaming and crying women and cursing and excited men, all sweeping toward me and Mrs. Sikkim.

13

I picked Mrs. Sikkim up in my arms. Over the heads of
several of the cast I saw the control men coming out of the
booth, so I guessed we weren't on the air any more. They'd
probably have cut us off sooner, only they were as much
enthralled by Mrs. Sikkim's confession as anybody else.
Somebody held the door open and I carried Mrs. Sikkim
out and followed one of the page boys into a huge audition
room down the hall. Against one wall there was a large
couch and I lowered her carefully onto it.

Someone must have kept his head, because I started
to say, "Get a doctor, somebody, will you?" and there one
was. He had his little black bag with him and went to work
right away.

It didn't take long. Mrs. Sikkim began to moan and stir
and then she sat up and looked around with wide, panic-
filled eyes. She looked toward the door and said, "Mr. Tinney . . . please, please, Mr. Tinney, help me."

I patted her shoulder and said, "Take it easy, Mrs. Sikkim, you'll be all right in a—"

A voice at my side, quiet but insistent, interrupted.
"Leave her alone, Shelley, you fool!"

I turned and almost needed a doctor myself.

Mr. Tinney was standing there with the package that
had come for him from Lisbon under his arm.

"Where did you come from?" I could scarcely speak.

"From home." He took Mrs. Sikkim's hand. "Mamie tried to tell me you were doing the program, but I found a package that had come for me and I wouldn't listen. She turned on the radio and I heard—but never mind, Shelley. I'll talk to you later. Just try to relax, Mrs. Sikkim. You shouldn't have done it. . . ."

"She didn't do it," I said. "She never killed him. She's just saying that to—"

"Quiet, Shelley!"

The room had been pretty well cleared, but now the door crashed open and heavy footsteps pounded across the carpet. A bull-like voice bellowed, "Where is that woman? Police brutality, eh? Goddammit, now I believe she did kill him. I'll find out where that letter opener—"

The doctor, turning, said, "Quiet, please."

I turned, too, and so did Mr. Tinney. I saw Taggert storming toward us. And he saw Mrs. Sikkim through the gap we'd made before the couch when she moved.

"Oh, there you are, Mrs. Sikkim. So you insist you did kill your husband."

Behind me I heard Mrs. Sikkim moan, "God, oh, please God—"

I stepped toward Taggert and said, "Wait a minute. Captain. You can't—"

He shoved me back with one hand. I lowered my head and charged and drove my left short but hard into the pit of his stomach. He bent over and said, "Ooof," and I stepped in close and brought up my right sharply. It only grazed the side of his face, and then he clubbed me with a powerful right sweep to the side of the head and I went over backwards and sidewards and the side of my head bopped on the floor.

I sat up, dizzily, and heard Mr. Tinney say, "Now cut out the roughhouse, Captain Taggert. This woman is in no condition—"

"She's in plenty good enough condition to get on the air and make a lot of charges against me and tell the world she killed her old man. I step out to the coffee pot for a quick cup of java because I'm dead from trying to get this Frangipanni to open up and I hear her saying how I pushed her kid around and—"

"Did you say you had Frangipanni down at headquarters?" asked Mr. Tinney.

"Yeah . . . but it's no good. He won't—"

Mr. Tinney looked at his wrist watch. "Come with me," he said. "He'll talk. When I show him what I have here he'll talk." He turned back to Mrs. Sikkim. "Please relax, Mrs. Sikkim, and don't worry about anything. Do as the doctor says and you'll be all right. I'll straighten everything out."

He patted her arm and nodded toward the doctor and started out. Taggert hesitated a minute, wondering whether he ought to follow or work on Mrs. Sikkim. He finally chased after Mr. Tinney. I wondered if I ought to stay and look after Mrs. Sikkim, but then I figured the doctor could handle it better than I could so I chased after Taggert.

In a back room at headquarters, Frieze and a couple of other detectives stood around a table at which Frangipanni sat. He still had on the same pepper-and-salt suit he'd worn when we saw him. The blood stains just looked like a couple of darker dirtier spots than the others he'd picked up in the meantime. He hadn't shaved in all that time either and the pupils of his eyes had fine red cobwebs spun all around them. The bandages weren't on his head any more.

Frieze saw us and exclaimed, "Mr. Tinney! Am I glad to see you! This guy hasn't said more than 'No' and 'I don't know' in two hours. He claims he left his joint right after you left him because he was afraid the same two guys would come back and try again to kill him. He wandered around some and wound up in a joint on the Bowery and just stayed there till we found him. He doesn't know anything about the notes or who killed Landry or Sikkim or Knight."

"Let me show him this," said Mr. Tinney. "I feel certain he'll tell us a number of interesting things about Mr. Sikkim and Mr. Landry and the notes."

Frangipanni looked at Mr. Tinney and at the package, and fright showed in his bloodshot eyes.

"May I have this chair?" asked Mr. Tinney. Frieze pushed it closer to the table, alongside Frangipanni, and Mr. Tinney sat down and opened up the package. Up till now Taggert had been making threatening noises at me and grumping about everybody and everything, but now he moved closer to Frangipanni and Mr. Tinney along with Frieze and the other cops.

Mr. Tinney pushed aside the wrapping paper and spread out one of the newspapers in the package. It was a Lisbon newspaper and the only thing I could make out was the date, June 6, 1931, and the three-column picture of the woman at the top center of the front page. The woman had long, black hair set in a lovely wave, and deep, dark eyes.

"That's the woman whose picture we found on Frangipanni!" said Frieze.

Frangipanni started to whimper and then to mutter what sounded like a prayer in some foreign language.

Mr. Tinney patted his trembling hand and said, "It's all right, Mr. Frangipanni. You won't have to talk. I'll tell the story. If I'm wrong you can correct me."

Frangipanni kept on muttering his prayer and occasionally whimpering.

"This, gentlemen," said Mr. Tinney, indicating the newspaper picture, "is Mr. Frangipanni's mother. Her name was Margot Dupre. Or at least that was her stage name. Her real name was Marguerite Deladet. She was married to a Portuguese perfumer-chemist named Henri Savoldi. They were very much in love and very happy, until Madame Savoldi met Amerandra Sikkim. Then she lost all interest in her husband and even in her son.

"She fell madly in love with Mr. Sikkim. After a time, however, Mr. Sikkim tired of her and told her he was through, that he wanted to have nothing more to do with her.

"She drank poison in her dressing room at the theater one night. As she toppled forward onto her dressing table, she knocked from it a bottle of the perfume which had, by virtue of its distinctiveness, become more or less her trademark. The odor of the perfume filled the room. It was a perfume especially prepared for her by her husband, one that was never made available or marketed commercially. It was, you might say, the odor of their love. It is very likely that Senhor Savoldi had made it for her originally in the early days of their courtship.

"Madame Savoldi did not die immediately. She lingered, suffering agonies which I cannot possibly describe to you. And her husband was at her bedside in those long hours before death finally took her. It is possible that he knew anyway that Mr. Sikkim was the cause of her suicide. He worked for Mr. Sikkim in a perfume distillery in Lisbon. But even if Senhor Savoldi didn't know it, his wife probably told him before she died.

"As soon as Mr. Sikkim learned of her suicide attempt, he fled the country; Senhor Savoldi swore revenge. He went mad with his desire for revenge. He left his job. He found out that Mr. Sikkim had gone to London. He followed him there but Mr. Sikkim got away again. He learned that Mr. Sikkim had fled to America. He followed again. By this time, however, his money had practically given out. He couldn't afford to buy passage for both his son and himself. . . ."

Mr. Tinney paused and looked at Frangipanni, who was staring at him with his mouth open and his jaws moving loosely.

"Is it correct so far, Mr. Frangipanni?" Mr. Tinney asked with a kindly tone in his voice.

Frangipanni nodded. "Yes," he said, "yes . . . you know all. But you do not know how he felt, my father, how the madness ate into his mind. How it made of him a strange and fearful animal, living only to kill. He carried with him a small bottle of the perfume. He sat with me in our rooms and held the bottle to his nose and to mine and said in a voice which was not his own, 'This is the odor, my son. The odor of love which has turned to hate. Not for my lovely Marguerite, but for the swine who killed her. I will kill him, my Charles, and if I do not, you must kill him!' He talked to me so for years. Every day! Every night!

"I was but a boy. I lived with this madman who was my father and the insanity crept into my own mind. When we came here to America it is true we had no money. I hid on the boat and my father brought me food, whatever was left over. I lived in almost complete darkness for nine days and as soon as we landed we came to the building where Sikkim had his place of business. My father instructed me to stay away from him, to walk far behind him. I was frightened. I wanted to run away but I could not. There was this thing we had to do. This swine we must kill."

He was looking directly at Mr. Tinney. I don't think he even knew the rest of us were in the room. He had felt in Mr. Tinney's recital of the facts a sympathy, an understanding which had not been shown him before. He spoke rapidly, excitedly, but with coherence.

"I saw my father shoot Sikkim. I saw the crowds and the policeman rush to him. I saw my father fight the policeman and—and the policeman was strong. He beat my father over the head and the face with his stick . . . and my father fell to the street, bloody and—and—"

Mr. Tinney reached over and put his hand on Frangipanni's.

"I wanted to help him," Frangipanni said, "but I was frightened. I was still but a boy. I watched them take my father away and I went away. I learned that the swine had not yet been killed, only wounded: My father they placed in an insane asylum. He died there. He had told me I must kill the man who had killed my mother. I would have, even if he had not so instructed me. I loved my mother—and my father. They were so happy . . . so . . . so . . . until Sikkim came into their lives and killed them. I was young but I knew that I must kill Sikkim. I knew that I must plan very carefully how I would kill him. I must kill him and not pay with my own life for doing it.

"I was without money, but I survived. After a time I found work, menial work, but enough to keep me alive. I worked hard and I saved the money which I earned and I studied in the schools at night. I worked out in my mind a plan. I would kill Sikkim, but before I did I would torture him with the memory of what he had done to my mother and father. Such a plan I knew would take much time, but I knew I must not hurry. I must work slowly and with care. My father had attempted to move quickly and he had died a slow, tortured death in a place for insane men.

"I studied perfumery and chemistry. I went to Italy after a number of years and established myself as Enrique Frangipanni. I even fostered the legend that I was a direct descendant of the famous Frangipanni family. So, after many more years I managed to come to the attention of Sikkim and I secured employment with him.

"My father had earlier passed on to me the formula for the perfume which he made for my mother. I sent Sikkim

the notes which threatened his death, saturated with the
odor. I wanted him to recall what he had done. I wanted
him to die a thousand times before I actually killed him.

"I sent to him two notes and had the others already
prepared to send to him. I was very careful. The notes I
wrote in a store which sells typewriters, when no sales person was looking. To make certain that he would remember
I drew beneath the notes a picture of a field of roses in
bloom . . . it is a sight which everyone who has been there
in the perfume industry associates with Lisbon.

"Sikkim knew to what the notes referred. He knew that
his death was near, but how near he did not know. I saw
the fear of dying grow stronger in his eyes day by day,
hour by hour. He did not know who it was who sent him
the notes. I had laid my plans with great care. My refer-
ences from Italy were beyond reproach.

"He did not know until he turned the notes over to
Landry to be investigated. Landry perhaps followed me,
saw me perhaps in the store which sells typewriters, pre-
paring my notes. Perhaps through some other means he
learned it was I who planned to murder Sikkim. He came
to me and told me he knew I was the sender of the notes.
He demanded that I pay. If I paid him much money, ten
thousand dollars, he would not tell Mr. Sikkim. I did not
believe him. I believed he would tell Mr. Sikkim in any
case whether I paid him the money or not. . . ."

Taggert couldn't hold out any longer. He leaned over
Frangipanni's shoulder and barked, "So you went to his
joint and killed him!"

Frangipanni's eyes widened and his head jerked up like
a man coming out of a dream. Terror showed in his eyes
again. He stared up at Taggert and raised his hands as if to
protect himself from a blow. Then he turned back to Mr.
Tinney and said, "Tell them, tell them, please, Mr. Tinney, that I did not kill Landry. . . please . . . please . . ."

Mr. Tinney looked at his wrist watch, got up out of his chair and walked away from the table, and Frieze moved away from us and followed him. Mr. Tinney whispered into Frieze's ear, and Frieze nodded his head; Mr. Tinney whispered something more and Frieze nodded again. Mr. Tinney walked back to the table.

"Gentlemen," he said, "Mr. Frangipanni is telling the truth. He did send the perfumed notes, but he did not kill Noel Landry, Amerandra Sikkim, or Jimmy Knight."

I stared at him with my mouth wide open. The room was full of open mouths, including Frieze's. He was as stunned as any of us. I wondered what Mr. Tinney had told him.

Mr. Tinney leaned over and patted Frangipanni's hand and said, "Good boy, you'll feel much better after this is all over."

He swung his cane with quite a jauntiness as he walked toward the door.

"Wait a minute," I yelled, "wait for me."

I started to race after him and Frieze jumped on me from behind and held me.

"Let go," I said, "I want to—"

"You're staying, Shell," Frieze said. "Mr. Tinney's orders."

Taggert finally recovered and bellowed at Mr. Tinney, "Hey! You can't do this. Whattaya mean he didn't kill those guys? You can't walk out of here."

Mr. Tinney, at the door, turned. "Captain Taggert," he said coldly, "I can walk out of here and I am going to. Mr. Frangipanni is not guilty of murder. You gentlemen have not resorted to any particularly vicious tactics as yet to make him confess. I assume that is because Captain Frieze held you all in check a bit. I want to warn you right now, Captain Taggert, that if I learn that you have laid a hand on Frangipanni I will cause him to sue you and the City of New York for more money than you will earn in the next fifty years. Remember that!"

He walked out. Frieze laughed so softly that I wouldn't have heard it if his mouth wasn't practically in my ear. Taggert, incredible as it might sound, was absolutely one hundred per cent speechless.

14

Frieze's laugh was soft and it died quickly. They took Frangipanni away, and fifteen minutes later Frieze and I were
stalking down the long hall on the twenty-eighth floor of
an apartment building.

"Just follow my lead," said Frieze, "and keep quiet." He
stopped before a door, placed his ear close to the jamb,
and listened. I edged up and listened, too. Voices came
faint but clear. One of them was Mr. Tinney's, the other a
woman's voice that I'd never heard before, and the third a
man's that was slightly familiar.

"Who—" I started to whisper.

"Ssshhh!" shushed Frieze.

We heard footsteps coming down the hall and we both
straightened up and turned quickly. It was a mailman. Frieze
trotted softly on the thick carpet and caught the mailman
fifteen feet from the door at which we'd been listening.
He grabbed the postman's arm, took his badge out of his
pocket, flashed it, and whispered something to the mailman, who whispered back. Then Frieze whispered again.

Frieze finally motioned me to come over from the door,
where I'd been standing like a dummy. I came and Frieze
moved me back and close to the wall. The mailman walked
up to the door of the apartment at which we'd been listening and pressed the buzzer. The door opened and a smooth

white arm reached out, took a package from the postman, signed the slip of paper he handed in, and withdrew. The door closed and the postman walked back toward us, looking a little less bewildered than I felt.

"What the—" I started to whisper again.

Frieze hissed for me to shut up as he led me back to the door. We pressed forward again.

"Open it now, please," Mr. Tinney was saying. "You'll find it quite interesting."

There was no answer, no sound that reached us at all for more than a minute. Then Mr. Tinney's voice again.

"I'll bet you hardly remember the occasion on which that picture was taken, do you, Willie Archibald?"

Still no other sound. Mr. Tinney had been speaking in his usual ultra-modulated voice and there wasn't really anything happening to make me jumpy, but I was—plenty! I had a terrific impulse to scream. I didn't. Because Mr. Tinney was talking again.

"I'll recall it for you, Willie. It was the evening after Brian O'Shannon's body was found in Lake Michigan. Mr. O'Shannon had been neatly stabbed to death before he was thrown into the lake. His death gave one Anthony Scappelli complete and undisputed control over all rackets in Chicago.

"Look at the picture, Willie. That's Mr. Scappelli with the large, fat face at the head of the table . . . and that dapper little fellow on his right—the guest of honor, apparently—is Willie Archibald. Willie disposed of Brian O'Shannon."

There was silence again and I felt my heart thumping against my chest. I started to get up, but Frieze grabbed my wrist and yanked me down again.

Then Mr. Tinney resumed. "You didn't have a mustache in those days, Willie, but aside from that you haven't changed much. You still wear those shirts which seem too large for you—those shirts so loose around the neck and especially at the cuffs!"

Finally, then, came the other man's voice, the one Mr. Tinney had been calling Willie Archibald. It was hard and cold and now I didn't recognize it at all. It didn't even sound familiar.

"I don't know what you're talking about, Mr. Tinney," it said.

"Oh, yes, you do, Willie. And it isn't doing you any good to tear that photograph. I've had several prints made of it. I even drew a mustache on one and you'd be surprised how little you've changed.

"That's your undoing, Willie. You really haven't changed at all. I have just come from a very interesting visit to one of the keys off the Florida coast. Lost Key, they call it. That's where Mr. Scappelli went into retirement when he got out of Alcatraz after serving his sentence on the income tax conviction. But, of course, you know all that.

"I had a little difficulty getting out to the island to see Mr. Scappelli. I finally had to resort to a little subterfuge. I put my collar on backwards and told them I was Father Mulcahy, a good friend of Father Trombino, who used to say mass in the little church Mr. Scappelli attended every Sunday even while he was engineering murders of scores of men.

"That got me in to see Mr. Scappelli quickly. You remember how religious he was, even in the days when you were his most proficient killer. You should. He remembers lots of little things about you—what a peculiar fascination perfumes always held for you, even in those days. He remembers how you used to come to the Cathedral Club and bring your little sweetheart, Mary O'Hara, the club cigarette girl, a new perfume almost every night. Mr. Scappelli told me you even prepared some of those perfumes yourself. Even then—"

He paused and again there was silence, until Mr. Tinney said, "Surely you remember that, Mrs. Roche. No girl ever forgets the early days of her courtship."

"Willie!" the girl's voice shrieked, "this old bastard's wise—"

And the man's voice grated, "Shut up, you fool!" Then came Mr. Tinney's softest chuckle, so soft it almost didn't make it through the door where we were listening.

"Mary O'Hara," he said, "you're forgetting you're a lady. You're the wife of Mr. Francis Roche, the perfume expert. Or maybe you're not forgetting. Maybe you don't have the poise and confidence Willie has because you know it's all over."

Again a pause and a silence as loud as a dynamite blast. And then Mr. Tinney, going on, "It *is* all over, Willie. I'd made up my mind some time ago that the counterfeit perfume racket was the real, underlying motive for these murders. I couldn't learn who was at the head of that enterprise. It might have been Mr. Sikkim himself, or Mr. Kerwin, for that matter. But I began to suspect you when I learned that that very lovely portrait of little Mary, which Sikkim had had painted with the intention of advertising *Morning's Laughter,* had never been used in any of the national advertising. You didn't want it used because you were afraid some of the old mob might recognize Mary's picture.

"Of course that was hardly enough to go on. But I'd wondered about the large shirts you wore, with the loose cuffs. It didn't seem right that a man who dressed so fastidiously in all other ways would wear such shirts. And then I read some very interesting true detective stories about the days of Mr. Scappelli's reign of terror in Chicago.

"And about Mr. Scappelli's number one killer, who always stabbed his victim to death. Those detective magazines really go into detail. They told that this killer used a jack-knife with a six-inch blade that flicked open at the press of a button and that was attached with a thick piece of rubber to a band the wielder wore on his forearm so that the knife could be snapped out of his sleeve and back again in a split second. The writer of this particular article was a Chicago crime reporter and he really knew his subject. But he didn't know that the most proficient wielder of this weapon, which I understand was quite standard equipment in the bloody gang days, was Willie Archibald, Scappelli's lieutenant in charge of the counterfeit bottle and label racket in those bootleg days."

Mr. Tinney was still speaking quite calmly, but now the slightest tremor of excitement began to creep into his voice. "Mr. Scappelli knew it, however, and he willingly told Father Mulcahy about it. Mr. Scappelli didn't know that his old friend, Willie Archibald, was now Francis Roche, respected perfumer, and he didn't know that Willie Archibald had reverted to type and killed Noel Landry because Landry had found out that he was at the head of the counterfeit perfume racket."

There was still no answer from Willie Archibald—or Roche or his wife. I nudged Frieze and gestured that I thought we ought to bust in. He shook his head.

Then Mr. Tinney's voice reached us again. "What did Landry do when he found out, Willie?" he asked. "Did he come to you and shake you down, as the detective magazines say, to keep him quiet? And then did he double-cross you and tell Mr. Sikkim, who originally hired him to make the investigation, that you were the racket king? Oh, all right, you don't have to answer. That's what I imagine happened, anyway. So Sikkim knew, and, being a very ruthless man, he thought he would take advantage of his knowledge. He called you in and told you that he didn't intend to expose you and have you arrested, but he probably told you you would have to stop counterfeiting Siquin perfumes, though you could continue to counterfeit the perfumes of his competitors . . . and possibly he even forced you to pay him to keep quiet."

His voice died out a little on the last word and I had a mental picture of Archibald-Roche poised like a leopard, ready to spring. Again I gestured to Frieze to bust in. And again he stopped me, although now he had his right hand resting lightly against the left lapel of his coat, ready to snatch at the gun in his holster.

Then Mr. Tinney said, "I see from your very tense attitude, Willie, that I have reconstructed the picture with a fair degree of accuracy. But that isn't all. I can tell you some more. You then learned that Landry was approaching still other perfume manufacturers and offering to sell them the name of the leader of the counterfeit perfume ring. You knew that one of these other manufacturers might 'buy' and, unlike Mr. Sikkim, might turn you over to the police.

"So there was really only one thing for you to do. You had to kill Noel Landry. But unfortunately for you, young Jimmy Knight had come there to collect for that frame-up photo of him and Carol and he saw you kill Mr. Landry. You saw him, too, but he got away from you that night. Then he went out to Mr. Sikkim's, after Mr. Landry was killed, to try to collect from Mr. Sikkim because Mr. Landry was dead and he had told Jimmy that Mr. Sikkim had ordered the photograph. You saw him that night and followed him to my home and when he started to write me that note you killed him."

Archibald-Roche had apparently collected himself somewhat, because he said now in his Roche voice, quiet and even, "That's all very fancy theorizing, Mr. Tinney. Even if Scappelli gave you that photograph of me at the banquet, and even if I did happen to have the misfortune to be associated with Mr. Scappelli in my youth, it hardly proves that I had anything to do with this counterfeit perfume racket, and it certainly does not prove that I killed either Landry or this Jimmy Knight you mention."

"No," said Mr. Tinney, "but the police have proof. In Mr. Landry's room at the Wilkins, right alongside the bed, they found a small piece of reddish rubber. I feel quite certain, since it isn't too easy to purchase that arm-band knife any more, that an adequate search of your apartment here will reveal the broken gadget. And the police laboratories will have no difficulty at all proving that the piece of rubber at the bedside comes from the same band as the one on your gadget, or any other good ones which you seem to keep so handy."

It happened fast, then. Archibald-Roche spoke harshly, gratingly, in his Archibald voice. "Very handy, Mr. Smart Man."

And before the last word was spoken there came the humming sound I knew so well. Then that stopped and I heard a chair slide back and the pounding of feet, just two or three short jumps, and something hard and heavy slamming to the floor and a high-pitched feminine scream that died in the middle.

I stood up and slammed my shoulder against the door. It didn't budge. I started to slam again and Frieze jerked me roughly away. His police positive was in his fist and he pointed it at the door's lock. Flame spurted in three small blasts accompanied by three sharp, cracking sounds so close they sounded like one. In the hallway the sound boomed back at us off the walls and ceiling.

Frieze stiff-armed the door and the smell of burning cordite bit into my nostrils as I plunged into the room after him. They were all mixed up and there was the glitter of steel in the lamplight and the red of blood. Mr. Tinney squirmed on the floor, trying to wrench his cane arm loose from the chair that had toppled over on him.

Archibald-Roche was trying to fling the chair from Mr. Tinney and stab him at the same time. Mary O'Hara Roche was trying to help her husband do the job, but she probably saved Mr. Tinney's life. As Roche brought the knife down in a vicious arc, she shoved her hand in the way trying to yank the chair off the old man. She let out a blood-curdling yell as knife bit into her forearm.

Frieze beat me to the tangle and shoved the gun in his hand up under Roche's chin so that his head snapped up hard.

"Drop the knife, Roche," he said, "or I'll blow your teeth right up through the top of your head."

Roche stood up and opened his fingers on the knife's handle but it didn't drop to the floor; it snapped up into his sleeve. Mr. Tinney, all the color drained from his face, clambered weakly to his feet, still holding his cane. His moulineting hadn't done him any good this time.

"Unstrap the knife, Shell," Frieze said.

The wide sleeve slid up easily and I unstrapped the band around his forearm. It was leather and it looked a lot like a wrist band, only it was larger and had this rubber contraption with the knife attached. The knife was still open and I hated to think what would have happened if that chair hadn't toppled over on Mr. Tinney when Archibald-Roche charged him.

Frieze handcuffed Willie and his wife together and to himself. With his left hand he snapped the knife shut and held it and the band in his palm.

"This is the same one. Here's the place where the piece of rubber was cut off or snapped off because it'd gotten rotten from not being used. It'll match up with the piece we've got all right."

I bent over and looked at Mary O'Hara Roche's arm.

"It's only a flesh wound," said Frieze. "Let it go. She should have got worse, alibiing for this rat."

Mr. Tinney felt he had to show us that he wasn't shaken. But his voice cracked in spots as he said, "You'll be able to find plenty of other proof that Roche is the murderer. If you'll check his bank accounts you'll probably notice some heavy cash withdrawals, and if you check Sikkim's you'll probably find correspondingly heavy cash deposits. . . ."

He was out of breath and couldn't go on. He didn't look or sound like anything but a very old and frightened man. I went over and took his arm and he said irritably and with a definite squeak in his voice, "Stop that, Shelley! I can walk by myself."

Frieze yanked the Roches over to the door and said, "I think I'll turn you two over to Taggert. He's been rarin' to work on somebody ever since he got into this. Taggert loves tough boys like you, Willie."

Roche said nothing. He glared at Mr. Tinney and Mr. Tinney said nervously, "Come on, Shelley. Let's be getting home. I'm a little tired."

As we walked out, Mary O'Hara Roche said, "You sneaky, nosey old—"

Frieze slammed the door shut after all of us. He took the killer and his wife away in a cab and Mr. Tinney and I got into our car.

I looked at my watch. It was exactly ten o'clock.

What Bill Catlett had called "The Hour of Des Tinney" would ordinarily just be coming to an end.

15

We headed uptown and I said, "You did it. You sure did it."

He said, "Be quiet, Shelley, please!"

Here was probably the greatest opportunity of his life to do some wholesale Grade-A bragging and he was passing it up! I stared at him. He had certainly had the hell scared out of him. I started to whistle happily.

"Shelley! Stop that idiotic whistling!"

I wondered if he was just too shaky to brag for the moment or whether some strange psychological thing had happened which had brought about a complete reform. Maybe he would never boast again.

I should have known better. He had three large glasses of that poisonous-looking vegetable stuff, while he listened to no less than nine Bing Crosby records. I was beginning to hate Crosby.

He was working on his fourth glass when he finally said, "Shelley, why did you attempt to do that broadcast yourself? And why, above everything else, did you permit Mrs. Sikkim to speak?"

His voice was perfectly modulated again and there wasn't a squeak or a crack in it. Now, I thought, was the time to find out whether he was ever going to brag again.

"Before we get into that," I said, "how did you find out about Scappelli living on that Florida—"

He didn't even give me a chance to finish the question. "I should think, Shelley," he interrupted, trying to sound greatly annoyed, "that everything would be obvious even to you by this time. I phoned the Chicago police. They've followed Mr. Scappelli's career with interest." He went on from there in great detail, repeating the things I'd heard him tell Willie Archibald, alias Roche.

I finally got in a question. "If you knew Roche was the murderer all along why did you put Frangipanni through that agony down at headquarters tonight? You certainly built up a case—"

"I'm sorry Mr. Frangipanni had to go through all that," Mr. Tinney said, "but I wanted to turn the police's attention, and Taggert's especially, to Mr. Frangipanni, so they would leave Mrs. Sikkim alone. I didn't want her harassed any more than she had been already."

"If you knew Roche was the murderer, why did you go to all the trouble of getting that stuff on Frangipanni?" I asked.

"I didn't know that Roche was the murderer at that time. I guessed that he might be the head of the counterfeit perfume racket. Someone else might have been the murderer and I felt it was necessary to thoroughly investigate every possibility. There were other persons who had ample motive for killing Mr. Landry and Mr. Sikkim who, I decided quite early in the investigation, was the key person to the whole case.

"For instance, there were the perfumed notes. They quite obviously were intended for and had been sent to Mr. Sikkim. We discovered quite early in our investigation that he had a distinct taste for illicit love affairs, that he was a ladies' man. The notes very plainly referred to love, a love which had turned to hatred. They referred also to the fact that a man and a woman had died. Wasn't it logical to assume that the person to whom the notes had been sent had caused the deaths of that man and woman? And doesn't that immediately suggest what is often called a triangle?"

"Yeah," I admitted, "all that was obvious."

"All that," said Mr. Tinney, putting his glass on the table, "and more. It was also apparent that the notes referred to a love affair which had taken place a number of years ago. Remember, the first note said something like 'Let the odor linger no longer in your nostrils . . .' That fact, too, pointed to Mr. Sikkim as the recipient. He was about fifty-five. Mr. Frangipanni, who tried to tell us that he received the notes, can hardly be thirty. He could scarcely have been mixed up in an illicit love affair over fifteen years ago.

"Then, all one had to do was ask oneself why did he say the notes had been sent to him? And the answer to that is simple. We had found the notes in his home. He had to put himself in the position of either the sender or the recipient of the notes. If he admitted he had sent them, he feared the police would get after him and give him the same sort of treatment they gave his father. You might have gathered from the fact that he ran away immediately after we warned him Captain Frieze would be coming to see him that he was mortally afraid of the authorities. You might have noticed that from the way he turned to me, as one who might understand his actions."

"I noticed that all right," I said. "He sure busted wide open when you started to tell that story. But how did you ever trace the love affair the notes talked about to Lisbon and how did you know when it happened?"

"That wasn't difficult. You recall the story Mrs. Sikkim told me about how she lost her arm. She didn't tell me that Mr. Sikkim had trampled her hand with his foot. That, to someone who didn't know Mr. Sikkim, would have sounded too incredibly cruel. She said it happened in an automobile accident, but she did admit that he rushed her out of Lisbon and the hospital there and to another country the day he trampled her hand. He wouldn't have done that unless he was afraid of something very serious, possibly scandalous, in which he might be involved. I reasoned that that something might very logically be the death of the woman with whom he had been having an affair. I even thought for a time he might have murdered the woman in a fit of passion.

"You know, of course, Shelley, that I have friends, people whom I have tried to help, in every part of the world. I simply cabled a friend in Lisbon to check the newspapers during the year 1931 for the death, either by suicide or murder, of a woman or a man. I pointed out in the cable that in all probability the death would tie in directly or indirectly with either a love affair or some kind of a strange perfume. As it happened, it was extremely easy for my Portuguese friend to find the case to which I referred. Margot Dupre was quite a famous actress in those days and her suicide rated the front page. And another thing which made it easy was that the perfume she always wore was mentioned quite prominently in the newspaper stories."

"It sounds simple," I said, "but you certainly did a job that would have made Sherlock Holmes turn green with envy. There's only one thing I still can't understand. With such a beautiful case against Frangipanni, how did you know he wasn't the murderer?"

"That was more obvious than anything else about the case," he said. "For one thing, Mr. Frangipanni was genuinely surprised when we told him that Mr. Landry had been killed. He didn't even know who had been murdered. You remember that before you blurted out to him that it was Mr. Landry he expressed great joy that the victim had been killed. He thought all the time we were talking that we were referring to Mr. Sikkim.

"Even more important, however, is the fact that Mr. Sikkim had already learned that Mr. Frangipanni had been sending him the notes and was planning to kill him. Those two thugs who were up in his apartment had been sent there by Mr. Sikkim to dispose of Mr. Frangipanni. You will recall when one of them asked who was at the door, I said, 'Mr. Sikkim,' and they opened it immediately. They thought it actually was the man who had hired them and therefore didn't hesitate to let him in. With Mr. Sikkim knowing of Mr. Frangipanni's intention to kill him, he would never let Mr. Frangipanni get close enough to him to permit an effective single stab of a knife to pierce his heart."

"I see," I said. "Sikkim didn't figure Roche was going to try to kill him and even if he did, Roche could handle that knife so fast, it was a cinch. As simple as the whole thing sounds, though, I take my hat off to you. If you're not the smartest man in the world, I don't know who is."

I poured it in and poured it in, and poured it in some more. A cat with a bowl of cream had nothing on Mr. Tinney. He lapped up the praise with every part of him. And what made it good was I really meant it. I did think he had done a terrific job. I knew this was the psychological moment.

"Wakely is all ready to apologize to you," I said finally. "He'll be around tomorrow morning some time. And I promise never to try to do the show myself again. And I'll apologize to Mrs. Sikkim for—"

"Oh, we all make mistakes, Shelley," he said benevolently. "I'm sure you meant well. And Mr. Wakely is coming up tomorrow, you say? That'll be fine."

Wakely came up. I saw to that, with the help of the morning papers. They were full of the show and how Mr.

Tinney had helped solve the murder. There were news stories and features and a couple of papers even had editorials on police brutality as charged by Mrs. Sikkim on the program. I knew we might have trouble with Taggert but I doubted it. Frieze had let him grab off a bigger hunk of credit for solving the case than he deserved. And I figured I could keep him from raising any fusses by telling him I might reveal how much he really had to do with catching the murderer. Anyway, the police brutality thing was practically lost in the shuffle with all the other angles of the case. Mr. Tinney and the program got the big play. We were worth a fortune of any sponsor's money and I knew it.

I called Wakely about eleven o'clock and his overenthusiastic greeting told me I was right. I greeted him back in a very worried tone.

"Look, Mr. Wakely," I said, "you started us on the air and I feel it's only right that I protect your interest in us. Mr. Tinney and I've been getting phone calls and wires all morning from agencies and sponsors, making us all kinds of crazy offers. I don't want to take any of them, but Mr. Tinney is a little peeved because of the demands you've been making for pre-broadcast scripts and rehearsals, and he didn't like the way you turned us down when I asked you for that measly ten thousand dollar advance. I think it would be a good idea if you came up and talked to him."

"I'll be over in an hour, Shelley," he said. "I appreciate your telling me all this. You'll help me talk sense to him, won't you?"

"Sure," I said, "I feel we owe it to you, Mr. Wakely."

He didn't need much help. He apologized and raised our price to twenty-five hundred and signed us for an additional twenty-six weeks with options. It was wonderful. Everything was wonderful with us and everybody else. Three months later, Ben and Carol Wills got married and Carol gave me a check for five thousand dollars made out to Mr. Tinney. Attached to the check was a little note which said:

> *In payment for a very satisfactory solution to a very difficult problem.*
> *Carol and Ben Sikkim.*

I thought that was that, until several weeks later. Carol and Ben were away on a honeymoon and we were having dinner with Mrs. Sikkim and Randolph Kerwin. After dinner, I excused myself and went out into the library and started to look over some of Ben's poetry books. He had a lot of good stuff.

After a while I became conscious of voices in the drawing room, adjoining the library.

"There's something," Mrs. Sikkim was saying. ". . . there's something I must tell you, Mr. Tinney. I won't feel . . ."

"I know, Katherine," Mr. Tinney said tenderly. "I know you killed Mr. Sikkim, just as you said you did, and that Randolph disposed of the letter-opener and prepared the note and put it into Mr. Sikkim's pocket to divert suspicion from you. I know you wanted to tell me you had killed him, even before the case was cleared up and . . . and Randolph persuaded you not to. I know all that and if I were you I would try very hard to forget it. You committed a crime, yes, but you were punished. You served your sentence—twenty-five years of it—before Mr. Sikkim died. And Willie Archibald *did* kill Noel Landry and Jimmy Knight. He was tried and convicted for Landry's murder. Let's just . . ."

I tiptoed to the bookcase and put back the book and went out the side door very quietly. I walked for a long time. The brisk breeze stung my cheeks . . . and brought tears to my eyes.

Print-on-demand titles available at
CoachwhipBooks.com

Ebook titles available at
Coachwhip.com

BRUTAL
Question

by
OLIVER WELD BAYER
author of
"AN EYE FOR AN EYE"

DEATH
BEATS
THE
BAND

IDA SHURMAN

MURDER AT DRAKE'S ANCHORAGE

E. LEE WADDELL

MAUDE PARKER

MURDER IN JACKSON HOLE

MURDER
AT GLEN ATHOL

NORMAN LIPPINCOTT

A strange clan—a grotesque dinner party—and
violent death in a little Pennsylvania town!

THE SERGEANT HARTY MYSTERIES

JOEL Y. DANE

MURDER CUM LAUDE
1
THE CABANA MURDERS

murder is mutuel

JACK DOLPH

Jack Dolph

MURDER MAKES THE MARE GO

TYLINE PERRY

THE OWNER
LIES DEAD

FRANCIS WALLACE

Little
HERCULES

A *Detective Novel* CLASSIC

A FULL LENGTH NOVEL

MEDORA
FIELD

WHO KILLED
AUNT MAGGIE?

BLOOD ON HER SHOE

MEDORA FIELD

THE CAT
SCREAMS
A HUGH RENNERT MYSTERY

TODD DOWNING

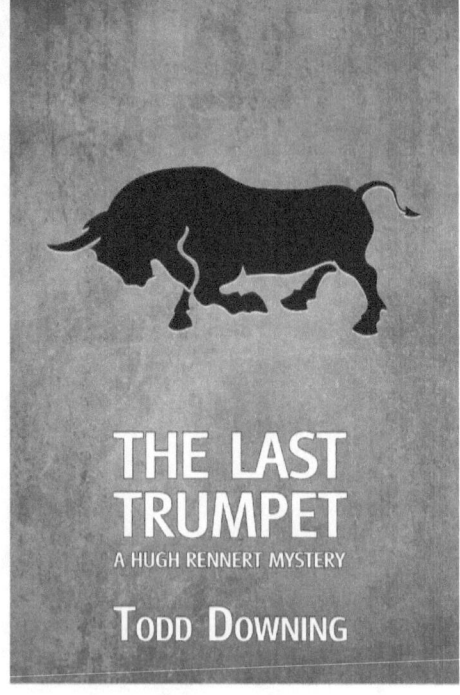

THE LAST
TRUMPET
A HUGH RENNERT MYSTERY

TODD DOWNING

HIDE AND GO SEEK

with, GOING TO ST. IVES

COLVER HARRIS

THE HOUSE THAT JACK BUILT

with, MURDER IN AMBER

COLVER HARRIS

THE
THING
IN THE
BROOK

PETER STORME

LAVERNE RICE
WELL DRESSED
FOR MURDER

www.ingramcontent.com/pod-product-compliance
Lightning Source LLC
Chambersburg PA
CBHW020614250626
47154CB00004B/1509